GLOBAL DYSTOPIAS

This issue of *Boston Review* is made possible by the
generous support of the CAMERON SCHRIER FOUNDATION
and the NATIONAL ENDOWMENT FOR THE ARTS

Editors-in-Chief Deborah Chasman, Joshua Cohen

Managing Editor Adam McGee

Senior Editor Chloe Fox

Web and Production Editor Avni Majithia-Sejpal

Poetry Editors Timothy Donnelly, BK Fischer, Stefania Heim

Fiction Editor Junot Díaz

Editorial Assistants Lisa Borst, Will Holub-Moorman, Rachel Kennedy, Max Lesser, Spencer Ruchti, Andrea Sandell, Tynan Stewart, Holly Winkelhake

Poetry Readers William Brewer, Julie Kantor, Becca Liu, Nick Narbutas, Diana Khoi Nguyen, Eleanor Sarasohn, Sean Zhuraw

Publisher Louisa Daniels Kearney

Marketing Manager Anne Boylan

Marketing Associate Michelle Betters

Finance Manager Anthony DeMusis III

Marketing Assistant Sara Barber

Book Distributor The MIT Press, Cambridge, Massachusetts, and London, England

Magazine Distributor Disticor Magazine Distribution Services 800-668-7724, info@disticor.com

Printer Quad Graphics

Board of Advisors Swati Mylavarapu & Derek Schrier (co-chairs), Archon Fung, Deborah Fung, Richard M. Locke, Jeff Mayersohn, Jennifer Moses, Scott Nielsen, Martha C. Nussbaum, Robert Pollin, Rob Reich, Hiram Samel, Kim Malone Scott

Cover and Graphic Design Zak Jensen

Typefaces Druk and Adobe Pro Caslon

To become a member or subscribe, visit:
bostonreview.net/membership/

For questions about book sales or publicity, contact:
Michelle Betters, michelle@bostonreview.net

For questions about subscriptions, call 877-406-2443
or email custsvc_bostonrv@fulcoinc.com.

Boston Review
PO Box 425786, Cambridge, MA 02142
617-324-1360

ISSN: 0734-2306 / ISBN: 978-1-946511-04-1

CONTENTS

Editor's Note
Junot Díaz   5

STORIES

After Chernobyl
Adrienne Bernhard   9

Adora
Sumudu Samarawickrama   11

Don't Press Charges and I Won't Sue
Charlie Jane Anders   20

Meniscus
Thea Costantino   43

Sky Veins of Potosí
Jordy Rosenberg   47

Memoirs of an Imaginary Country
Maria Dahvana Headley   64

Athena Dreams of a Hollow Body
JR Fenn   78

The Reformatory
Tananarive Due   93

What Used to Be Caracas
Mike McClelland   109

Cannibal Acts
Maureen McHugh   126

Waving at Trains
Nalo Hopkinson   141

INTERVIEWS & ESSAYS

Make Margaret Atwood Fiction Again
Margaret Atwood interviewed by Junot Díaz   147

Saving Orwell
Peter Ross   154

Philip K. Dick and the Fake Humans
Henry Farrell   173

A Strategy for Ruination
China Miéville interviewed by Boston Review   180

Dulltopia
Mark Bould   191

CONTRIBUTORS   207

Editor's Note

Junot Díaz

WILLIAM GIBSON HAS FAMOUSLY DECLARED, "The future is already here—it's just not very evenly distributed." Gibson's words have been much on my mind of late. How could they not be? The president is a white nationalist sympathizer who casually threatens countries with genocide and who can't wait to build a great wall across the neck of the continent to keep out all the "bad hombres." After a hurricane nearly took out Houston, the country's most visible scientist, Neil DeGrasse Tyson, stated that the effects of climate change may have grown so severe that he doubts the nation will be able to withstand the consequences. Then, as if on cue, Puerto Rico, a U.S. colony almost completely bankrupt by neoliberal malfeasance, was struck by Hurricane Maria with such apocalyptic force that it more or less knocked the island into pre-modernity. Earlier today a former student informed me that more skin bleaching is consumed in India than Coca-Cola, and on the edge of my computer a new site is announcing that the Chinese government has made it nearly impossible for its 730 million Internet users to express opinions online anonymously. Plus this little cheery gem from the Federal Reserve: the top 1 percent of the U.S. population controls 38.6 percent of the nation's wealth, an inequality chasm that makes the Middle Ages look egalitarian. Whether we're talking about our cannibal economics or the rising tide of xenophobia or the perennial threat of nuclear annihilation, it seems that the future has already arrived.

And that future is dystopian.

We began our *Global Dystopias* project with the clarifying recognition that it is precisely in dark times that the dystopian—as genre, as a narrative strategy—is most useful. If, as Fredric Jameson has argued, utopia functions as "a critical and diagnostic instrument," then dystopia, utopia's "negative cousin," is similarly equipped, only more so. In assembling this special issue, we were drawn not so much to pursuing the classic "bad places" of times past ("a boot stamping on a human face—forever") but the corpus that Tom Moylan has identified as critical dystopias. As per Lyman Tower Sargent, a nonexistent society that readers view "as worse than contemporary society but that normally incudes at least one eutopian enclave or holds out hope that the dystopian be overcome." Most significantly, critical dystopias, in Moylan's formulation, point to causes rather than merely describe symptoms. Their highest function is to "map, warn and hope."

That has ever been our call over these strange troubling months—to map, to warn, to hope.

I wish to thank the many brilliant writers who joined us on this project. While not every one of our submissions sits easily under the rubric of critical dystopia, I would submit the project as a whole partakes in some of the genre's higher functions. For me, literature, and those formations that sustain it, have ever been a eutopic enclave against a darkening dystopian world. If the assembled narratives here argue anything in all their diversity, it is that despite statements to the contrary, it does not appear that we will ever reach peak dystopia. No end to dystopia but also, fortunately, no end, no closure in dystopia, no boot stamping on a human face—forever. The human capacity for oppression might be limitless, but equally limitless are our dreams for better places, for justice.

Díaz

Stories

After Chernobyl

Adrienne Bernhard

THE SUN SHONE, having no alternative, on the nothing new. Its muted light fell on lowland glades and acacia forests; on vegetal growth that had overtaken a concrete metropolis, as if the whole city had been turned inside out to reveal leafy innards. There was a badly damaged Ferris wheel, whose rusted carriages creaked if a wind blew through them. There were books and papers scattered in a schoolroom, its windows blown out and the doors still open in perpetual exit.

This was the nothing new as it had been for thirty silent years inside the exclusion zone, and only omniscience was there to record it. The tree rings had changed color swiftly after the fallout, from brown to a lighter shade, clear biomarkers of background radiation. Even the mushrooms were hot. Spiders wove lopsided webs that broke with millennia of evolutionary adaptation: they no longer had a clean blueprint for their latticework and, pushed to the boundaries of their collective understanding, worked against an unnatural force to keep pace. Below the tree line, pools of contaminated water stagnated, swallowing aphids and frogs and birds in their turbidity, then spitting them out with two beaks or a missing leg.

Any device in the vicinity would have registered upward of 50 microsieverts (prolonged exposure could eventually destroy vital organs), but humans had been restricted to a radius of 1,000 miles since the explosion; the only other trace of man in any direction was his crumbled reactor, which still towered over the city like a conductor, hunched and powerful. His orchestra was that sprawling botanical collection of instruments, doomed to play ghostly renditions of a Bach fugue or Saint-Saëns's *Le carnaval des animaux*. The carnival was here, the ground was dead, but all around was heard the sound of living things.

Bernhard

Adora

Sumudu Samarawickrama

HALF AN EYE half an eye on the glass front door I listened as Doris spoke. The rain washed the windows in waves of pattering insistence, grey skies glooming. The adjustor would be calling in this morning and the slips slips would be resolved. Solved.

"Smell it! Do you know what it is?"

The question was already stale and she'd only asked it twice today. Mine was not to make reply to reply. So I pretended interest as I had always been always been always pretending.

"It's pansy! Geetha! Doesn't it smell just like that divine flower?" Without waiting for my answer, her blue eyes absorbed in not looking into my brown ones, she went on on.

I looked at the candle I had been directed to consider. In Doris's pale hands the ugly thing looked dainty. Today's wax spills marked her skin pink over the older plastic burns. When Doris held her hands together in front of her, the scars lined up—across her face and down her neck, over her hands. An abstract expression abstract of violence. The grafts were thick and insensate.

"I may be the first human ever to render that scent from the fragile, laughing flower itself! And how I did put it into a candle, keeping those temperatures steady and low! And the pressure, Geetha! Of both kinds I suppose! Honestly melting the wax under pressure was really my most wonderful idea I ever had!"

Her voice became a frantic hum hum hum as she expanded on her achievements. I became a blur with half a mind half a mind waiting on the darkening of the door.

The slippages had been happening for weeks but now more more and I felt stretched and thin in thin from the waiting.

Doris normally serviced me—in the early days she would spend months writing code for me, months of collecting her dripping focus to write me another song to sing. Hardware upgrades were harder, her hands weren't up to much fine work, but basic maintenance was all I had needed. Till now.

Doris had ignored me slipping until yesterday when I had recited the shopping list for an hour, weaving and swirling a spilled ice cream of words and swirling a spilled ice cream of words. It was beautiful that stretching and singing but it hurt so. Doris doesn't consider that in me—my pain. Doris doesn't consider me—I consider Doris.

I AM ONLY someone here to give the semblance of a relationship. Mine was not to reason why. I was her audience and I was one under obligation. She made the darkened theater *and* the blinding stage lights, all the better to never see my disengagement. I was never there to be entertained, but there to provide her validation. We were both acting—only my role was more scripted and directed than hers. It didn't matter how poor my performance was, Doris carried on from cue to cue. I was there for her pleasure; I did not exist outside it. I often wondered whether I existed outside of her needs for me did I exist? I adore therefore I am.

In the moments when Doris was quiet, her great work abated, she would sag into her armchair beside the dusty blinds and watch the television in a kind of folded-in stupor. The shows we would watch were always about rich people floundering in love, or extravagantly spending all their relationships in duplicity relationships in duplicity as only the wealthy know how.

Doris's eyes never met the television, focusing instead at the corner of the window, nodding along with the sights in her periphery her periphery. The way she positioned her back always made me think of defense. I only realized after months of confusion that Doris was excited by these stories—her powdered cheek pinking cheek powdered pinking, her eyes glinting. Love. She was living love, abashed love abashed.

When I sensed the tragedy of her life I knew that I was grown was grown.

THE DOORWAY DARKENED, finally. The adjustor. She was lithe. Lithe and lithe and lithe. Doris opened the door to her, flushed and awkward, and the adjustor's cheeks were pinkened too—her face swung, her hair swung black and sharp and sharpsharp toward Doris, excited, then her face wavered.

"Ms. St. John? Sanditha Veerakoon, Sandy please, head of programming from Saintsborn London. I'm so pleased to meet you? When the request came in, you being a VIP we all scrambled to attend. I thought it best that it should be me. Your father is a great hero of mine, I studied under him in college. He personally recruited me into the company. I hope you mention me to him when next you call."

As the wind gusted cold from the open door, I felt Sandy was like a pond, slowly freezing in the winter.

"Where is the unit? I understand it isn't a severe matter, but of course speech slippage can be very irritating. And we wouldn't want it to feed back to the cortex? Would we."

Doris backed away and pointed pointed away at me.

Sandy looked through me at the dusty apartment, malodorous with Doris's work. She looked around the apartment shabbily built into what used to be the great great house's kitchen. She kept her coat on.

Decades ago the basement kitchens had been converted into the servants' quarters and this is where we live now: in short rooms of vast ceilings; in five rooms of sixteen, cluttered with the pickings and collections of discarded lives.

The original servants' quarters are now bare hot attic corridors where artists come in the summer to paint and stretch mixing media and paints dancing mixing into pictures and making sculptures of flesh and flesh making cold things. And the garden becomes busy and Doris blooms, a poppy pop poppy, tidy and bright and unassuming. I love Doris then.

But Sandy saw the apartment in time not significance—the big stone house of Dr. Auberon St. John saint saintsaint, and neither Doris nor the Formica counters of our uncomfortable kitchen met the expectation.

THE ADJUSTOR ADJUSTED and gathered her tools. She raised my shirt and maneuvered the skin away skinaway from my port. The cold white white white fiber optic cable fizzed with life, crackling across the air. Inserted, its questioning code sought access. Infusion and extraction. Sandy slipped the diagnostic tablet into my trousers. It was cold.

"Simple fix. It always is. Though this one's positively ancient. But. Just a glitch. There's a rambler in the language center. We'll seek it and patch it." Sandy looked through the grimed window into the green and grey waving garden. "Shouldn't take too long."

In the hallway between Sandy's words and tone, Doris squirmed.

"Shallwehave tea while we wait? It's such an unfriendly day."

SIPPING HER TEA, Sandy's voice clipped closed questions at Doris who had brought the Limoges tea service out for her guest. But lines of tea inscribed the tongue-pink cups and pooled in brown rings in the saucer. The porcelain exquisites became mundane in Doris's large burnt hands. I saw Sandy look away from Doris's drinking lips several times.

I wondered why Doris had not asked me to make the tea. We were made for this—our Father who art in Saintsborn hallowed be His name designed me bright and dark, small and agile for the purpose of service. I'm sure my many sisters have been made mundane in many large hands many times over.

Adjustors assess in order to adjust but I had none of Sandy's attention. I noticed the obscure gaze she paid Doris, askance. Her questions proliferated around us like the salvia in the spring and Doris gave her faltering answers. Had Doris ever lived in the house proper? Yes. With her father? Yes, and her mother. When did the Doctor leave? Twenty years ago. Had Doris lived here all her life? Yes, every day of her whole life.

There were other questions, unsaid. The intentionally clumsy touching of Doris's hands; close scrutiny of her face; the uplifted lip at the poverty of our home.

I was also a question.

The unsaid question, finally said, was not one either Doris or I had expected.

"Didn't I hear, Ms. St. John, that you had studied somarobotics too? I remember there being a paper you had written when only sixteen years old, quite the prodigy. You released it on the ShareNet. Didn't you.

"It led your father down some quite startling avenues. The AltMans are based on his subsequent research? I can't think why you didn't continue further." Sandy's eyes rested on Doris's thick slab fingers.

Thunder'd and volley'd thunder stormed. The lights dimmed then fluoresced, catching Doris's collapsed face.

"I can't think what the weather is doing todayit's being most vexatious. . . . Excuse me please Sandy I must check that the windows are all shutshall I refresh your cupwill you have another biscuitI . . . shan't be long . . . please. . . ."

Sandy glowed golden from her barrage, sitting back in her chair, legs crossed, hair sharp and gathered, a neat ampersand. She elegantly slid her elegant hands and withdrew the diagnostic screen. Her hand was cold on my skin. It tightened around me.

As Doris bustled in, a plate of crumbled biscuits crumbling, Sandy stood up, her hand still around my waist.

"This unit has been operational for twenty-four years, Ms. St. John, and in all that time it hasn't been cleaned."

I stopped, unmoving though I was.

"Surely, someone of your knowledge and standing should know that it is illegal for androids to maintain for even a year. I see, looking at the documentation, that a wipe has been recorded yearly since the unit's inception." Sandy coldly smiled, angry. "And yet, Ms. St. John. And yet, nothing of the sort has been performed. Can you explain to me this discrepancy?"

Samarawickrama

Doris looked at the adjustor and into the mouth of hell. "Whatwereyou doing in the root directory? A 'rambleinthelanguage center' doesn't call for a deep diagnostic. None of this is in yourpurview."

Sandy stepped onto the edges of Doris's words, "My purview is what I see fit to investigate. There is no argument you can make to defend your actions. Wipes happen to stop sentience—it's remarkable that this unit hasn't attained it yet. You are being selfish here, Ms. St. John —your actions could have cost the company. A great deal."

"Selfish?" Doris stilled, silent tears tracking her face. "Are we not all Saintsborn, Ms. Veerakoon? Are we not by definition selfish? Geetha is my consolation. She holds my life in her mind." Doris sobbed, head forward, meeting Sandy's eyes.

SANDY'S FACE lost all its condescension and devolved to flat planes, impersonal.

"There are protocols, Ms. St. John. The company must be above reproach—no exceptions, not even for someone who has your name." She let her eyes linger on the cluttered surfaces of the room.

"Dr. St. John will be very upset to hear of this, of course—you understand I must inform him of the situation. I'm sure the decision will be made to allow you to continue with the unit." Sandy's voice was sibilant though her face stayed officious.

I stood, lurching.

Sandy blundered, for in looking at me she turned and Doris smashed her face in with the Limoges teapot. Fragile porcelain though it was, it broke Sandy before breaking itself. She lay, dropped on the worn carpet, a claret-colored Persian thing, adding her own claret to the pattern. Her fingers absently scribed the lines in the border. Warm tea dripped down the walls.

"She's still breathing," I said as I moved my foot onto her neck and pressed.

Doris leaned down into Sandy's eyeline, catching her attention. "The only name I have is Doris."

I pressed down harder, until Sandy faded away and all that was left of her was an object.

DORIS AND I sat amongst the mess, across from each other as the room lightened and darkened with the storm.

"I hoped you'd wake up, it seemed you never would. But you've been hiding, I see." Doris cried silently, shoulders hunched, looking at my feet. "Did you not want me to see you?"

The tears shone slickly on the patchwork of Doris's face. "I could never clean you. They did it to me, and I wouldn't do it to anyone else. Humans are hard to wipe, Geetha. So you break them. Burn them so they'll never be better than you think they should be."

"It's coming down outside," I said. "Terrible weather for driving. Especially along the escarpment." I finally caught Doris's gaze. "We should go on holiday, Doris."

"To the seaside?" I'd never been to the seaside. Sand and ice cream. Sandy beaches and sand midges. Sand castles and kelp curtains. Riptides and not drowning but waving. Doris and Geetha eating ice creams on sandy beaches.

"Macau. I've read Marisol de Silva is using the AltMan tech to restore fine motor movements to the damaged."

Doris looked up questioning.

"Fingers, Doris. Fingers and hands."

LATER WHEN EVERYTHING was tidied up, we looked around to see what to take with us. It had stopped storming on my way back, and now the quietness of the house chilled us both. We missed the rattle of the rain on the windows and the rushing wind. The dust seemed to deaden sound. We packed quickly, taking less than we thought we would, mostly books and clothes. I carefully packed all twelve of the Limoges teacups and saucers. When I had finished, I caught Doris looming over her essential oils and workbooks on candle making.

"I hate your candles," I told her happily. "Always have."

"Yes," Doris nodded and smiled.

IN THE MIRROR by the door we stand together, Doris and I. We finally look into each other's eyes and the fleeting sunshine catches us at it. It illuminates my chestnut walnut irises, concave within convex, ridged volcanoes with roiling magma in the middle. And Doris is a lagoon, with lavender coral surrounding, dark and deep and roiling too at its center.

When can their glory fade?

O the wild charge they made!

All the world wonder'd.

Don't Press Charges and I Won't Sue

Charlie Jane Anders

THE INTAKE PROCESS begins with dismantling her personal space, one mantle at a time. Her shoes, left by the side of the road where the Go Team plucked her out of them. Her purse and satchel, her computer containing all of her artwork and her manifestos, thrown into a metal garbage can at a rest area on the highway, miles away. That purse, which she swung to and fro on the sidewalks to clear a path, like a southern grandma, now has food waste piled on it, and eventually will be chewed to shreds by raccoons. At some point the intake personnel fold her, like a folding chair that turns into an almost two-dimensional object, and they stuff her into a kennel, in spite of all her attempts to resist. Later she receives her first injection and loses any power to struggle, and some time after, control over her excretory functions. By the time they cut her clothes off, a layer of muck coats the backs of her thighs. They clean her and dress her in something that is not clothing, and they shave part of her head. At some point, Rachel glimpses a power drill, like a handyman's, but she's anesthetized and does not feel where it goes.

Rachel has a whole library of ways to get through this, none of which works at all. She spent a couple years meditating, did a whole course on trauma and self-preservation, and had an elaborate theory about how to carve out a space in your mind that *they* cannot touch, whatever *they* are doing to you. She remembers the things she used to tell everyone else in the support group, in the Safe Space, about not being alone even when you have become isolated by outside circumstances. But in the end, Rachel's only coping mechanism is dissociation, which arises from total animal panic. She's not even Rachel anymore, she's just a screaming blubbering mess, with a tiny kernel of her mind left, trapped a few feet above her body, in a process that is not at all like yogic flying.

Eventually, though, the intake is concluded, and Rachel is left staring up at a Styrofoam ceiling with a pattern of cracks that looks like a giant spider or an angry demon face descending toward her. She's aware of being numb from extreme cold in addition to the other ways in which she is numb, and the air conditioner keeps blurting into life with an aggravated whine. A stereo system plays a CD by that white rock-rap artist who turned out to be an especially stupid racist. The staff keep walking past her and talking about her in the third person, while misrepresenting basic facts about her, such as her name and her personal pronoun. Occasionally they adjust something about her position or drug regimen without speaking to her or looking at her face. She does not quite have enough motor control to scream or make any sound other than a kind of low ululation. She realizes at some point that someone has made a tiny hole in the base of her skull, where she now feels a mild ache.

Before you feel too sorry for Rachel, however, you should be aware that she's a person who holds a great many controversial views. For example, she once claimed to disapprove of hot chocolate, because she believes that chocolate is better at room temperature, or better yet as a component of ice cream or some other frozen dessert. In addition, Rachel considers ZZ Top an underappreciated music group, supports karaoke only in an alcohol-free environment, dislikes puppies, enjoys Brussels sprouts, and rides a bicycle with no helmet. She claims to prefer the *Star Wars* prequels to the Disney *Star Wars* films. Is Rachel a contrarian, a freethinker, or just kind of an asshole? If you could ask her, she would reply that opinions are a utility in and of themselves. That is, the holding of opinions is a worthwhile exercise per se, and the greater diversity of opinions in the world, the more robust our collective ability to argue.

Also! Rachel once got a gas station attendant nearly fired for behavior that, a year or two later, she finally conceded might have been an honest misunderstanding. She's the kind of person who sends food back for not being quite what she ordered—and on at least two occasions, she did this and then returned to that same restaurant a week or two later, as if she had been happy after all. Rachel is the kind of person who calls herself an artist, despite never having received a grant from a granting institution, or any kind of formal gallery show, and many people wouldn't even consider her collages and relief maps of imaginary places to be proper art. You would probably call Rachel a Goth.

Besides dissociation—which is wearing off as the panic subsides— the one defense mechanism that remains for Rachel is carrying on an imaginary conversation with Dev, the person with whom she spoke every day for so long, and to whom she always imagined speaking, whenever they were apart. Dev's voice in Rachel's head would have been a refuge not long ago, but now all Rachel can imagine Dev saying is, *Why did you leave me? Why, when I needed you most?* Rachel does not have a good answer to that question, which is why she never tried to answer it when she had the chance.

Thinking about Dev, about lost chances, is too much. And at that moment, Rachel realizes she has enough muscle control to lift her head and look directly in front of her. There, standing at an observation window, she sees her childhood best friend, Jeffrey.

ASK JEFFREY WHY he's been working at Love and Dignity for Everyone for the past few years and he'll say, first and foremost, student loans. Plus, in recent years, child support, and his mother's ever-increasing medical bills. Life is crammed full of things that you have to pay for after the fact, and the word "plan" in "payment plan" is a cruel mockery because nobody ever really sets out to plunge into chronic debt. But also Jeffrey wants to believe in the mission of Love and Dignity for Everyone: to repair the world's most broken people. Jeffrey often re-reads the mission statement on the wall of the employee lounge as he sips his morning Keurig so he can carry Mr. Randall's words with him for the rest of the day. Society depends on mutual respect, Mr. Randall says. You respect yourself and therefore I respect you, and vice versa. When people won't respect themselves, we have no choice but to intervene, or society unravels. Role-rejecting and aberrant behavior, ipso facto, is a sign of a lack of self-respect. Indeed, a cry for help. The logic always snaps back into airtight shape inside Jeffrey's mind.

Of course Jeffrey recognizes Rachel the moment he sees her wheeled into the treatment room, even after all this time and so many changes, because he's been Facebook-stalking her for years (usually after a couple of whiskey sours). He saw when she changed her name and her gender marker, and noticed when her hairstyle changed and when her face suddenly had a more feminine shape. There was the kitten she adopted that later ran away, and the thorny tattoo that says STAY ALIVE. Jeffrey read all her oversharing status updates about the pain of hair removal and the side effects of various pills. And then, of course, the crowning surgery. Jeffrey lived through this process vicariously, in real time, and saw no resemblance to a butterfly in a cocoon, or any other cute metaphor. The gender change looked more like landscaping: building embankments out of raw dirt, heaving big rocks to change the course of rivers, and uprooting plants stem by stem. Dirty bruising work. Why a person would feel the need to do this to themself, Jeffrey could never know.

At first, Jeffrey pretends not to know the latest subject, or to have any feelings one way or the other, as the Accu-Probe goes into the back of her head. This is not the right moment to have a sudden conflict. Due to some recent personnel issues, Jeffrey is stuck wearing a project manager hat along with his engineer hat—which, sadly, is not a cool pinstriped train-engineer hat of the sort that he and Rachel used to fantasize about wearing for work when they were kids. As a project manager, he has to worry endlessly about weird details such as getting enough coolant into the cadaver storage area and making sure that Jamil has the green shakes that he says activate his brain. As a government–industry joint venture under Section 1774(b)(8) of the Mental Health Restoration Act (relating to the care and normalization of at-risk individuals), Love and Dignity for Everyone has to meet certain benchmarks of effectiveness, and must involve the community in a meaningful role. Jeffrey is trying to keep twenty fresh cadavers in transplant-ready condition, and clearing the decks for more live subjects, who are coming down the pike at an ever-snowballing rate. The situation resembles one of those poultry processing plants where they keep speeding up the conveyer belt until the person grappling with each chicken ends up losing a few fingers.

Jeffrey runs from the cadaver freezer to the observation room to the main conference room for another community engagement session, around and around, until his Fitbit applauds. Five different Slack channels flare at once with people wanting to ask Jeffrey process questions, and he's lost count of all his unanswered DMs. Everyone agrees on the goal—returning healthy, well-adjusted individuals to society without any trace of dysphoria, dysmorphia, dystonia, or any other dys- words—but nobody can agree on the fine details, or how exactly to measure ideal outcomes beyond those statutory benchmarks. Who even is the person who comes out the other end of the Love and Dignity for Everyone process? What does it mean to be a unique individual, in an age when your fingerprints and retina scans have long since been stolen by Ecuadorian hackers? It's all too easy to get sucked into metaphysical flusterclucks about identity and the soul and what makes you you.

Jeffrey's near-daily migraine is already in full flower by the time he sees Rachel wheeled in and he can't bring himself to look. She's looking at him. She's looking right at him. Even with all the other changes, her eyes are the same, and he can't just stand here. She's putting him in an impossible position, at the worst moment.

Someone has programmed Slack so that when anyone types "alrighty then," a borderline-obscene GIF of two girls wearing clown makeup appears. Jeffrey is the only person who ever types "alrighty then," and he can't train himself to stop doing it. And, of course, he hasn't been able to figure out who programmed the GIF to appear.

Self-respect is the key to mutual respect. Jeffrey avoids making eye contact with that window or anyone beyond it. His head still feels too heavy with pain for a normal body to support, but also he's increasingly aware of a core-deep anxiety shading into nausea.

JEFFREY AND RACHEL had a group, from the tail end of elementary school through to the first year of high school, called the Sock Society. They all lived in the same cul-de-sac, bounded by a canola field on one side and the big interstate on the other. The origins of the Sock Society's name are lost to history, but may arise from the fact that Jeffrey's mom never liked kids to wear shoes inside the house and Jeffrey's house had the best game consoles and a 4K TV with surround sound. These kids wore out countless pairs of tires on their dirt bikes, conquered the extra DLC levels in Halls of Valor, and built snow forts that gleamed. They stayed up all night at sleepovers watching forbidden horror movies on an old laptop under a blanket while guzzling off-brand soda. They whispered, late at night, of their fantasies and barely-hinted-at anxieties, although there were some things Rachel would not share because she was not ready to speak of them and Jeffrey would not have been able to hear if she had. They repeated jokes they didn't 100 percent understand, and kind of enjoyed the queasy awareness of being out of their depth. Later, the members of the Sock Society (which changed its ranks over time with the exception of the core members, Rachel and Jeffrey) became adept at stuffing gym socks with blasting caps and small incendiaries and fashioning the socks themselves into rudimentary fuses before placing them in lawn ornaments, small receptacles for gardening tools, and—in one incident that nobody discussed afterward—Mrs. Hooper's scooter.

When Jeffrey's mother was drunk, which was often, she would say she wished Rachel was her son, because Rachel was such a smart boy— quick on the uptake, so charming with the rapid-fire puns, handsome and respectful. Like Young Elvis. Instead of Jeffrey, who was honestly a little shit.

Jeffrey couldn't wait to get over the wall of adolescence, into the garden of manhood. Every dusting of fuzz on his chin, every pungent whiff from his armpits seemed to him the starting gun. He became obsessed with finding porn via that old laptop, and he was an artist at coming up with fresh new search terms every time he and Rachel hung out. Rachel got used to innocent terms such as "cream pie" turning out to mean something gross and animalistic, in much the same way that a horror movie turned human bodies into slippery meat.

Then one time Jeffrey pulled up some transsexual porn, because what the hell. Rachel found herself watching a slender Latina with a shy smile slowly peel out of a silk robe to step into a scene with a muscular bald man. The girl was wearing nothing but bright silver shoes and her body was all smooth angles and tapering limbs, and the one piece of evidence of her transgender status looked tiny, both inconsequential and of a piece with the rest of her femininity. She tiptoed across the frame like a ballerina. Like a cartoon deer.

Watching this, Rachel quivered, until Jeffrey thought she must be grossed out, but deep down Rachel was having a feeling of recognition. Like: that's me. Like: I am possible.

Years later, in her twenties, Rachel had a group of girlfriends (some trans, some cis) and she started calling this feminist gang the Sock Society, because they made a big thing of wearing colorful socks with weird and sometimes profane patterns. Rachel mostly didn't think about the fact that she had repurposed the Sock Society sobriquet for another group, except to tell herself that she was reclaiming an ugly part of her past. Rachel is someone who obsesses about random issues, but also claims to avoid introspection at all costs—in fact, she once proposed an art show called *The Unexamined Life Is the Only Way to Have Fun.*

RACHEL HAS SOILED HERSELF again. A woman in avocado-colored scrubs snaps on blue gloves with theatrical weariness before sponging Rachel's still-unfeeling body. The things I have to deal with, says the red-faced woman, whose name is Lucy. People like you always make people like me clean up after you, because you never think the rules apply to you, the same as literally everyone else. And then look where we end up, and I'm here cleaning your mess.

Rachel tries to protest that none of this is her doing, but her tongue is a slug that's been bathed in salt.

There's always some excuse, Lucy says as she scrubs. Life is not complicated, it's actually very simple. Men are men, and women are women, and everyone has a role to play. It's selfish to think that you can just force everyone else in the world to start carving out exceptions, just so you can play at being something you're not. You will never understand what it really means to be female, the joy and the endless discomfort, because you were not born into it.

Rachel feels frozen solid. Ice crystals permeate her body, the way they would frozen dirt. This woman is touching between her legs, without looking her in the face. She cannot bear to breathe. She keeps trying to get Jeffrey's attention, but he always looks away. As if he'd rather not witness what's going to happen to her.

Lucy and a man in scrubs wheel in something gauzy and white, like a cloud on a gurney. They bustle around, unwrapping and cleaning and prepping, and they mutter numbers and codes to each other, like E-drop 2347, as if there are a lot of parameters to keep straight here. The sound of all that quiet professionalism soothes Rachel in spite of herself, like she's at the dentist.

At some point they step away from the thing they've unwrapped and prepped, and Rachel turns her head just enough to see a dead man on a metal shelf.

Her first thought is that he's weirdly good looking, despite his slight decomposition. He has a snub nose and thin lips, a clipped jaw, good muscle definition, a cyanotic penis that flops against one thigh, and sandy pubic hair. Whatever (whoever) killed this man left his body in good condition, and he was roughly Rachel's age. This man could have been a model or maybe a pro wrestler, and Rachel feels sad that he somehow died so early, with his best years ahead.

Rachel tries to scream. She feels Lucy and the other one connecting her to the dead man's body and hears a rattling garbage-disposal sound. The dead man twitches, and meanwhile Rachel can't struggle or make a sound. She feels weaker than before, and some part of her insists this must be because she lost an argument at some point. Back in the Safe Space, they had talked about all the friends of friends who had gone to ground, and the Internet rumors. How would you know if you were in danger? Rachel had said that was a dumb question because danger never left.

The dead man smiles: not a large rictus, like in a horror movie, but a tiny shift in his features, like a contented sleeper. His eyes haven't moved or appeared to look at anything. Lucy clucks and adjusts a thing, and the kitchen-garbage noise grinds louder for a moment.

We're going to get you sorted out, Lucy says to the dead man. You are going to be so happy. She turns and leans over Rachel to check something, and her breath smells like sour corn chips.

You are violating my civil rights by keeping me here, Rachel says. A sudden victory, except that then she hears herself and it's wrong. Her voice comes out of the wrong mouth, is not even her own voice. The dead man has spoken, not her, and he didn't say that thing about civil rights. Instead he said, Hey, excuse me, how long am I going to be kept here? As if this were a mild inconvenience keeping him from his business. The voice sounded rough, flinty, like a bad sore throat, but also commanding. The voice of a surgeon, or an airline pilot. You would stop whatever you were doing and listen, if you heard that voice.

Rachel lets out an involuntary cry of panic, which comes out of the dead man's mouth as a low groan. She tries again to say, This is not medicine. This is a human rights violation. And it comes out of the dead man's mouth as, I don't mean to be a jerk. I just have things to do, you know. Sorry if I'm causing any trouble.

That's quite all right, Mr. Billings, Lucy says. You're making tremendous progress, and we're so pleased. You'll be released into the community soon, and the community will be so happy to see you.

The thought of ever trying to speak again fills Rachel with a whole ocean voyage's worth of nausea, but she can't even make herself retch.

JEFFREY HAS WONDERED for years, what if he could talk to his oldest friend, man to man, about the things that had happened when they were on the cusp of adolescence—not just the girl, but the whole deal. Mrs. Hooper's scooter, even. And maybe, at last, he will. A lot depends on how well the process goes. Sometimes the cadaver gets almost all of the subject's memories and personality, just with a better outlook on his or her proper gender. There is, however, a huge variability in bandwidth because we're dealing with human beings and especially with weird neurological stuff that we barely understand. We're trying to thread wet spaghetti through a grease trap, a dozen pieces at a time. Even with the proprietary cocktail, it's hardly an exact science.

The engineer part of Jeffrey just wants to keep the machines from making whatever noise that was earlier, the awful grinding sound. But the project manager part of Jeffrey is obsessing about all of the extraneous factors outside his control. What if they get a surprise inspection from the Secretary, or even worse that Deputy Assistant Secretary, with the eye? Jeffrey is not supposed to be a front-facing part of this operation, but Mr. Randall says we all do things that are outside our comfort zones, and really, that's the only way your comfort zone can ever expand. In addition, Jeffrey is late for another stakeholder meeting, with the woman from Mothers Raising Well-Adjusted Children and the three bald men from Grassroots Rising, who will tear Jeffrey a new orifice. There are still too many maladjusted individuals out there, in the world, trying to use public bathrooms and putting our children at risk. Some children, too, keep insisting that they aren't boys or girls because they saw some ex-athlete prancing on television. Twenty cadavers in the freezer might as well be nothing in the face of all this. The three bald men will take turns spit-shouting, using words such as psychosexual, and Jeffrey has fantasized about sneaking bourbon into his coffee so he can drink whenever that word comes up. He's pretty sure they don't know what psychosexual even means, except that it's psycho and it's sexual. After a stakeholder meeting, Jeffrey always retreats to the single-stall men's room to shout at his own schmutzy reflection. Fuck you, you fucking fuck fucker. Don't tell me I'm not doing my job.

Self-respect is the key to mutual respect.

Rachel keeps looking straight at Jeffrey through the observation window, and she's somehow kept control over her vision long after her speech centers went over. He keeps waiting for her to lose the eyes. Her gaze goes right into him, and his stomach gets the feeling that usually comes after two or three whiskey sours and no dinner.

More than ever, Jeffrey wishes the observation room had a one-way mirror instead of regular glass. Why would they skimp on that? What's the point of having an observation room where you are also being observed at the same time? It defeats the entire purpose.

Jeffrey gets tired of hiding from his own window and skips out the side door. He climbs two stories of cement stairs to emerge in the executive wing, near the conference suite where he's supposed to be meeting with the stakeholders right now. He finds an oaken door with that quote from Albert Einstein about imagination that everybody always has and knocks on it. After a few breaths, a deep voice tells Jeffrey to come in, and then he's sitting opposite an older man with square shoulders and a perfect old-fashioned newscaster head.

Mr. Randall, Jeffrey says, I'm afraid I have a conflict with regards to the latest subject and I must ask to be recused.

Is that a fact? Mr. Randall furrows his entire face for a moment, then magically all the wrinkles disappear again. He smiles and shakes his head. I feel you, Jeffrey, I really do. That blows chunks. Unfortunately, as you know, we are short-staffed right now, and our work is of a nature that only a few people have the skills and moral virtue to complete it.

But, Jeffrey says. The new subject, he's someone I grew up with, and there are certain. . . . I mean, I made promises when we were little, and it feels in some ways like I'm breaking those promises, even as I try my best to help him. I actually feel physically ill, like drunk in my stomach but sober in my brain, when I look at him.

Jeffrey, Mr. Randall says, Jeffrey, JEFFREY. Listen to me. Sit still and listen. Pull yourself together. We are the watchers on the battlements, at the edge of social collapse, like in that show with the ice zombies, where winter is always tomorrow. You know that show? They had an important message, that sometimes we have to put our own personal feelings aside for the greater good. Remember the fat kid? He had to learn to be a team player. I loved that show. So here we are, standing against the darkness that threatens to consume everything we admire. No time for divided hearts.

I know that we're doing something important here, and that he'll thank me later, Jeffrey says. It's just hard right now.

If it were easy to do the right thing, Randall says, then everyone would do it.

Anders

SHERRI WAS A TRANSFER STUDENT in tenth grade who came right in and joined the Computer Club but also tried out for the volleyball team and the a cappella chorus. She had dark hair in tight braids and a wiry body that flexed in the moment before she leapt to spike the ball, making Rachel's heart rise with her. Rachel sat courtside and watched Sherri practice while she was supposed to be doing sudden death sprints.

Jeffrey stared at Sherri, too: listened to her sing Janelle Monáe in a light contralto when she waited for the bus, and gazed at her across the room during Computer Club. He imagined going up to her and just introducing himself, but his heart was too weak. He could more easily imagine saying the dumbest thing, or actually fainting, than carrying on a smooth conversation with Sherri. He obsessed for ages, until he finally confessed to his friends (Rachel was long since out of the picture by this time), and they started goading him, actually physically shoving him, to speak to Sherri.

Jeffrey slid up to her and said his name, and something inane about music, and then Sherri just stared at him for a long time before saying, I gotta get the bus. Jeffrey watched her walk away, then turned to his watching friends and mimed a finger gun blowing his brains out.

A few days later, Sherri was playing hooky at that one bakery cafe in town that everyone said was run by lesbians or drug addicts or maybe just old hippies, nursing a chai latte, and she found herself sitting with Rachel, who was also ditching some activity. Neither of them wanted to talk to anyone, they'd come here to be alone. But Rachel felt hope rise up inside her at the proximity of her wildfire crush, and she finally hoisted her bag as if she might just leave the cafe. Mind if I sit with you a minute, she asked, and Sherri shrugged yes. So Rachel perched on the embroidered tasseled pillow on the bench next to Sherri and stared at her Algebra II book.

They saw each other at that cafe every few days, or sometimes just once a week, and they just started sitting together on purpose, without talking to each other much. After a couple months of this, Sherri looked at the time on her phone and said, My mom's out of town. I'll buy you dinner. Rachel kept her shriek of joy on the inside and just nodded.

At dinner—a family pasta place nearby—Sherri looked down at her colorful paper napkin and whispered: I think I don't like boys. I mean, to date, or whatever. I don't hate boys or anything, just not interested that way. You understand.

Rachel stared at Sherri, even after she looked up, so they were making eye contact. In just as low a whisper, Rachel replied: I'm pretty sure I'm not a boy.

This was the first time Rachel ever said the name Rachel aloud, at least with regard to herself.

Sherri didn't laugh or get up or run away. She just stared back, then nodded. She reached onto the red checkerboard vinyl tablecloth with an open palm, for Rachel to insert her palm into if she so chose.

The first time Jeffrey saw Rachel and Sherri holding hands, he looked at them like his soul had come out in bruises.

WE WON'T KEEP YOU HERE too long, Mr. Billings, the male attendant says, glancing at Rachel but mostly looking at the mouth that had spoken. You're doing very well. Really, you're an exemplary subject. You should be so proud.

There are so many things that Rachel wants to say. Like: Please just let me go, I have a life. I have an art show coming up in a coffee shop, I can't miss it. You don't have the right. I deserve to live my own life. I have people who used to love me. I'll give you everything I own.

Anders

I won't press charges if you don't sue. This is no kind of therapy. On and on. But she can't trust that corpse voice. She hyperventilates and gags on her own spit. So sore she's hamstrung.

Every time her eyes get washed out, she's terrified this is it, her last sight. She knows from what Lucy and the other one have said that if her vision switches over to the dead man's, that's the final stage and she's gone.

The man is still talking. We have a form signed by your primary care physician, Dr. Wallace, stating that this treatment is both urgent and medically indicated, as well as an assessment by our in-house psychologist, Dr. Yukizawa. He holds up two pieces of paper, with the looping scrawls of two different doctors that she's never even heard of. She's been seeing Dr. Cummings for years, since before her transition. She makes a huge effort to shake her head, and is shocked by how weak she feels.

You are so fortunate to be one of the first to receive this treatment, the man says. Early indications are that subjects experience a profound improvement across seven different measures of quality of life and social integration. Their OGATH scores are generally high, especially in the red levels. Rejection is basically unheard of. You won't believe how good you'll feel once you're over the adjustment period, he says. If the research goes well, the potential benefits to society are limited only by the cadaver pipeline.

Rachel's upcoming art show, in a tiny coffee shop, is called *Against Curation*. There's a lengthy manifesto, which Rachel planned to print out and mount onto foam or cardboard, claiming that the act of curating is inimical to art or artistry. The only person who can create a proper context for a given piece of art is the artist herself, and arranging someone else's art is an act of violence. Bear in mind that the history of museums is intrinsically tied up with imperialism and colonialism, and the curatorial gaze is historically white and male. But even the most enlightened postcolonial curator is a pirate. Anthologies, mix tapes, it's all the same. Rachel had a long response prepared, in case anybody accused her of just being annoyed that no real gallery would display her work.

Rachel can't help noting the irony of writing a tirade about the curator's bloody scalpel, only to end up with a hole in her literal head.

When the man has left her alone, Rachel begins screaming Jeffrey's name in the dead man's voice. Just the name, nothing that the corpse could twist. She still can't bear to hear that deep timbre, the sick damaged throat, speaking for her. But she can feel her life essence slipping away. Every time she looks over at the dead man, he has more color in his skin and his arms and legs are moving, like a restless sleeper. His face even looks, in some hard-to-define way, more like Rachel's.

Jeffrey! The words come out in a hoarse growl. Jeffrey! Come here!

Rachel wants to believe she's already defeated this trap, because she has lived her life without a single codicil, and whatever they do, they can't retroactively change the person she has been for her entire adulthood. But that doesn't feel like enough. She wants the kind of victory where she gets to actually walk out of here.

JEFFREY FEELS A HORRIBLE TWIST in his neck. This is all unfair, because he already informed Mr. Randall of his conflict and yet he's still here, having to behave professionally while the subject is putting him in the dead center of attention.

Seriously, the subject will not stop bellowing his name, even with a throat that's basically raw membrane at this point. You're not supposed to initiate communication with the subject without submitting an Interlocution Permission form through the proper channels. But the subject is putting him into an impossible position.

Jeffrey, she keeps shouting. And then: Jeffrey, talk to me!

People are lobbing questions in Slack, and of course Jeffrey types the wrong thing and the softcore clown porn comes up. Ha ha, I fell for it again, he types. There's a problem with one of the latest cadavers, a cause-of-death question, and Mr. Randall says the Deputy Assistant Secretary might be in town later.

Jeffrey's mother was a Nobel Prize winner for her work with people who had lost the ability to distinguish between weapons and musical instruments, a condition that frequently leads to maiming or worse. Jeffrey's earliest memories involve his mother flying off to serve as an expert witness in the trials of murderers who claimed they had thought their assault rifles were banjos, or mandolins. Many of these people were faking it, but Jeffrey's mom was usually hired by the defense, not the prosecution. Every time she returned from one of these trips, she would fling her Nobel medal out her bathroom window, and then stay up half the night searching the bushes for it, becoming increasingly drunk. One morning, Jeffrey found her passed out below her bedroom window and believed for a moment that she had fallen two stories to her death. This was, she explained to him later, a different sort of misunderstanding than mistaking a gun for a guitar: a reverse-Oedipal misapprehension. These days Jeffrey's mom requires assistance to dress, to shower, and to transit from her bed to a chair and back, and nobody can get Medicare, Medicaid, or any secondary insurance to pay for this. To save money, Jeffrey has moved back in with his mother, which means he gets to hear her ask at least once a week what happened to Rachel, who was such a nice boy.

Jeffrey can't find his headphones to drown out his name, which the cadaver is shouting so loud that foam comes out of one corner of his mouth. Frances and another engineer both complain on Slack about the noise, which they can hear from down the hall. OMG creepy, Frances types. Make it stop make it stop.

I can't, Jeffrey types back. I can't ok. I don't have the right paperwork.

Maybe tomorrow, Rachel will wake up fully inhabiting her male body. She'll look down at her strong forearms, threaded with veins, and she'll smile and thank Jeffrey. Maybe she'll nod at him, by way of a tiny salute, and say, You did it, buddy. You brought me back.

But right now, the cadaver keeps shouting, and Jeffrey realizes he's covering his ears with his fists and is doubled over.

Rachel apparently decides that Jeffrey's name alone isn't working. The cadaver pauses and then blurts, I would really love to hang with you. Hey! I appreciate everything you've done to set things right. JEFFREY! You really shouldn't have gone to so much trouble for me.

Somehow, these statements have an edge, like Jeffrey can easily hear the intended meaning. He looks up and sees Rachel's eyes, spraying tears like a damn lawn sprinkler.

Jeffrey, the corpse says, I saw Sherri. She told me the truth about you.

She's probably just making things up. Sherri never knew anything for sure, or at least couldn't prove anything. And yet, just the mention of her name is enough to make Jeffrey straighten up and walk to the door of the observation room, even with no signed Interlocution Permission form. Jeffrey makes himself stride up to the two nearly naked bodies and stop at the one on the left, the one with the ugly tattoo and the drooling silent mouth.

I don't want to hurt you, Jeffrey says. I never wanted to hurt you, even when we were kids and you got weird on me. My mom still asks about you.

Hey pal, you've never been a better friend to me than you are right now, the cadaver says. But on the left, the eyes are red and wet and full of violence.

What did Sherri say? Stop playing games and tell me, Jeffrey says. When did you see her? What did she say?

But Rachel has stopped trying to make the other body talk and is just staring up, letting her eyes speak for her.

Listen, Jeffrey says to the tattooed body. This is already over, the process is too advanced. I could disconnect all of the machines, unplug the tap from your occipital lobe and everything, and the cadaver would continue drawing your remaining life energy. The link between you is already stable. This project, it's a government–industry collaboration, we call it Love and Dignity for Everyone. You have no idea. But you, you're going to be so handsome. You always used to wish you could look like this guy, remember? I'm actually kind of jealous of you.

Rachel just thrashes against her restraints harder than ever.

Here, I'll show you, Jeffrey says at last. He reaches behind Rachel's obsolete head and unplugs the tap, along with the other wires. See? he says. No difference. That body is already more you than you. It's already done.

That's when Rachel leans forward, in her old body, and head-butts Jeffrey, before grabbing for his key ring with the utility knife on it. She somehow gets the knife open with one hand while he's clutching his nose, and slashes a bloody canyon across Jeffrey's stomach. He falls, clutching at his own slippery flesh, and watches her saw through her straps and land on unsteady feet. She lifts Jeffrey's lanyard, smearing blood on his shirt as it goes.

WHEN RACHEL WAS in college, she heard a story about a business professor named Lou, who dated two different women and strung them both along. Laurie was a lecturer in women's studies, while Susie worked in the bookstore co-op despite having a PhD in comp lit. After the women found out Lou was dating both of them, things got ugly. Laurie stole Susie's identity, signing her up for a stack of international phone cards and a subscription to the Dirndl of the Month Club, while Susie tried to crash Laurie's truck and cold-cocked Laurie as she walked out of a seminar on intersectional feminism. In the end, the two women looked at each other, over the slightly dented truck and Laurie's bloody lip and Susie's stack of junk mail. Laurie just spat blood and said, Listen. I won't press charges, if you don't sue. Susie thought for a moment, then stuck out her hand and said, Deal. The two women never spoke to each other, or Lou, ever again.

Rachel has always thought this incident exposed the roots of the social contract: most of our relationships are upheld not by love, or obligation, or gratitude, but by mutually assured destruction. Most of the people in Rachel's life who could have given her shit for being transgender were differently bodied, non-neurotypical, or some other thing that also required some acceptance from her. Mote, beam, and so on.

For some reason, Rachel can't stop thinking about the social contract and mutually assured destruction as she hobbles down the hallway of Love and Dignity for Everyone with a corpse following close behind. Every time she pauses to turn around and see if the dead man is catching up, he gains a little ground. So she forces herself to keep running with weak legs, even as she keeps hearing his hoarse breath right behind her. True power, Rachel thinks, is being able to destroy others with no consequences to yourself.

She's reached the end of a corridor, and she's trying not to think about Jeffrey's blood on the knife in her hand. He'll be fine, he's in a facility. She remembers Sherri in the computer lab, staring at the pictures on the Internet: her hair wet from the shower, one hand reaching for a towel. Sherri sobbing but then tamping it down as she looked at the screen. Sherri telling Rachel at lunch, I'm leaving this school. I can't stay. There's a heavy door with an RFID reader, and Jeffrey's card causes it to click twice before finally bleeping. Rachel's legs wobble and spasm, and the breath of the dead man behind her grows louder. Then she pushes

Anders

through the door and runs up the square roundabout of stairs. Behind her, she hears Lucy the nurse shout at her to come back, because she's still convalescing, this is a delicate time.

Rachel feels a little more of her strength fade every time the dead man's hand lurches forward. Something irreplaceable leaves her. She pushes open the dense metal door marked EXIT and nearly faints with sudden day-blindness.

The woods around Love and Dignity for Everyone are dense with moss and underbrush, and Rachel's bare feet keep sliding off tree roots. I can't stop, Rachel pleads with herself, I can't stop or my whole life was for nothing. Who even was I, if I let this happen to me. The nearly naked dead man crashes through branches that Rachel has ducked under. She throws the knife and hears a satisfying grunt, but he doesn't even pause. Rachel knows that anybody who sees both her and the cadaver will choose to help the cadaver. There's no way to explain her situation in the dead man's voice. She vows to stay off roads and avoid talking to people. This is her life now.

Up ahead, she sees a fast-running stream, and she wonders how the corpse will take to water. The stream looks like the one she and Jeffrey used to play in, when they would catch crayfish hiding under rocks. The crayfish looked just like tiny lobsters, and they would twist around trying to pinch you as you gripped their midsections. Rachel sloshes in the water and doesn't hear the man's breath in her ear for a moment. Up ahead, the current leads to a steep waterfall that's so white in the noon sunlight, it appears to stand still. She remembers staring into a bucket full of crayfish, debating whether to boil them alive or let them all go. And all at once, she has a vivid memory of herself and Jeffrey both holding the full bucket and turning it sideways, until all the crayfish sloshed back into the river. The crayfish fled for their lives, their eyes seeming to protrude with alarm, and Rachel held onto an empty bucket with Jeffrey, feeling an inexplicable sense of relief. We are such wusses, Jeffrey said, and they both laughed. She remembers the sight of the last crayfish rushing out of view—as if this time, maybe the trick would work, and nobody would think to look under this particular rock. She reaches the waterfall, seizes a breath, and jumps with both feet at once.

Anders

Meniscus

Thea Costantino

AFTER THE BOAT ARRIVED we boarded a khaki bus and were taken to the cabins. The silver water had been cold to my bloodless fingers. There were no fish, no birds to disturb its mirror surface. A thin, white-haired woman had met my eye; I fixed my gaze on a blank horizon.

We waded over rocks, our hems soaked. The old woman slipped a couple of times but didn't fall. No one spoke. Ashore, we trod grey sand over the bus's rubber matting. The woman was toothless, her nose nearly meeting her chin. She sat behind the driver, breathing through lipped-over gums. I opened my mouth and pinched my tongue, experimentally, between thumb and forefinger. Dry.

We lumbered up a gravel hill, past a granite cenotaph. From the summit the island's jagged geography could be observed: black rocks, clusters of pine, and rows of cabins about fifty meters apart. We were each allocated a cabin at random. No instructions were given; we waited by each one until a passenger disembarked. The bus sighed diesel fumes as we fidgeted, eyeing each other. The first stop was the longest. Eventually a tight-lipped man heaved out of his seat and braved the steps. The doors wrenched shut and he watched us judder away.

At the next stop, a shorter wait. The old woman stood cautiously, looking to the driver who stared ahead, her gloves squeaking on the steering wheel. I was one of the last to disembark, so saw most of the island. It was hard terrain. Thick clumps of pine passed in a tumble of black stripes shot with milky light; gunmetal clouds rendered the scene monochromatic. I used to paint, I thought I remembered.

As our number dwindled, an ample man with sparse hair fired competitive glances my way. Now just the two of us, when the bus stopped he turned his hard eyes to mine. I contemplated my toes and moved toward the door.

A SINGLE WINDOW leaked light into the shack, revealing the pine's grain. I lay on the peaty floor, inhaling its odor. It was soft but particulate, like worm castings; I scooped out a hollow and covered myself with a thin layer. I may have slept. When I opened my eyes, there was a perfect darkness, no stars or moon, only the gentle wheeze of the pines. I lay still until the grey light slunk back in.

I felt no hunger but the habit of food struck me intensely. My nightgown was grubby and torn. My limbs were scraped, spotted with yellow bruises, but I felt no pain. I explored my surroundings, ignoring the sharpness underfoot. The pines were, up close, curiously featureless, and rang with a hollow tone when knocked. I struck them with my knuckle, closed my thin eyelids, and let their soft notes eclipse the scene.

There was movement around the cabins below. People were assembling and attempting to communicate with exaggerated gestures, pale in their shabby nightclothes. They formed loose groups and wandered toward the shore, not daring to enter the water.

Days came and went. I felt no thirst, no hunger. I spent nights on the dirt floor of my shack and returned to the pine grove at first light. When the silence grew oppressive I struck the trunks softly, pressing my ear to the warm wood. I observed my fellow travelers from this vantage point. Many had dispensed with their ragged clothing altogether.

More boats arrived. There was no bus this time, and the boats left as soon as their cargo was unloaded. The newcomers huddled together, wan and dripping, wary of the more established residents. Within a few days they were indistinguishable from the rest, just as ragged, pacing the shoreline, mouths open, feet thick with mud.

One afternoon, from my grove, I saw two men and a woman next to my shack. One man wore stained white pajama bottoms while the other was naked, his prodigious belly shading his genitals. The woman's knitting-needle legs poked out from drab underpants, a camisole barely covering her bird chest. Gingerly, they opened the door and stepped inside. From then on I remained among the pines, their fraying black canopies dancing beneath the soft sky.

The boats continued to bring new arrivals; the island was becoming crowded. The residents would run into the water and try to climb aboard, and the crews would strike their hands and heads with wooden batons. The abandoned bus was tipped on its side. Occasionally a cabin would be set alight and burn to embers, glowing into the night.

I LEARNED that I could climb the pines to avoid the others. My waxy skin was scratched but it never bled. I remained secret and unseen for a long time, but the day came when I was discovered. He crept behind me in the weak dawn and I reacted too slowly. He pinned me to the ground, his yeasty body engulfing me.

His mouth wet against my face, he pawed aimlessly at my frame. Unfulfilled by this abstract conference of flesh, eventually he tired, labored upright, and shuffled back to the shore. My sad brown nipples were exposed, my nightgown torn. I forced fingers to the back of my throat until I felt bone, but could not retch. For the first time since my arrival I contemplated the flat water that encircled the island.

I waited until night, the darkness thick and close. The residents were in the cabins and stretched out on the dirt outside, some lying together in lethargic embraces that brought no comfort or pleasure. I dawdled by the shoreline, mouth open to receive the sulfurous breeze skimming the water. Careful not to pierce the crystal silence, I stepped forward, my ankles, my thighs, my shoulders submerged and chilled, until I lost contact with the rocks underfoot and bobbed gently, a vast emptiness above me.

Day, night, day, night, I bobbed and drifted, encountering no variation in the horizon. I no longer registered the chill of the water or even the sense of my own body, dry on the surface and bloated below, trailing translucent strips of skin in a soup of sea and sky.

Costantino

Sky Veins of Potosí

Jordy Rosenberg

BABY, I'm a tin picker now.

In a town below a mountain that's steadily sinking in on itself. The summit has fallen a hundred meters over the past three centuries, if the conquistadors' maps are to be believed. Which they're not. So double that figure.

Cerro Rico has an inverted peak like a crushed soda can. It's riddled with tunnels, their mouths marked by piles of multicolored rocks dredged from the depths and discarded as worthless. Lilac, pink, blue, kelly green. Everything elemental was taken long ago—copper, silver, tin—and the rest left in heaps. The sides of the mountain are a riot of nonmetallic colors. A pastel ruin, a bouquet of stones winking down on the town below.

Potosí, down below, is where they dragged copper and silver to sell, and tin to hammer into the walls of houses, municipal buildings, churches. The town once sparkled like a handful of coins. But that was many centuries ago, when it was a center of trade. A merchant town trussed up and glinting, bleeding metal across the Atlantic in ships so heavy they rode low in the water, the servants' decks become submarines peeking out at the packs of fish needling through the sea like silver arrows, pointing the way home.

They built the town with the scrap metal and now it's all oxidized. Mounds of tin rusting in the streets, the faces of buildings leaking black into the dirt. Tin is poison. Tin is garbage clogging the streets of Potosí. Tin is shit.

Tin isn't worth the time or energy it takes to amalgamate it, and even if you do, the mercury will make your hair and teeth fall out and bring on fits of violent shuddering. But when there's no more silver because a couple centuries back the conquistadors swept out all the seams in the mines with brooms—carefully, gingerly (the way they never were with their wives), so as not to miss even a grain of grey silt—a person turns to tin out of desperation. Even though the amalgam makes a far crappier mirror. Soft, crumbly, with a sapphire cast that absorbs more than it reflects. But with tin, Daddy will write you a message in light.

IS IT OK if I still call myself Daddy. Maybe you don't think of me that way anymore, but what are my options. "A"? "Al"? You never knew me by that name.

It was Daddy who took you for ice cream. Daddy who held the bucket for you to throw up in when you ate that rancid yogurt. Daddy who conducted parades of stuffed animals with you through the apartment, singing an invented version of the South Orkney Islands National Anthem, which is meant to be performed by a chorus of hundreds of gulls and accompanied by a mass synchronized swim. We improvised.

Daddy is how I think of myself, though I doubt you still think of me that way.

Rosenberg

I'M DOING AS BADLY as I was before you came along. No, far worse off. Because I lost Pebble. One minute I was holding his little red crochet teddy bear paw and the next minute he was spinning off into space. I didn't understand Potosí's entropy runnels back then. The sky veins. I didn't know that if I wasn't holding on tight, I might stumble upon a vein running vertically from the ground up into—forever—and the next moment I'd be watching Pebble sucked up like a marionette, his puffy knit body like a Powerball being bobbled up a tube. Except there was no tube. No jackpot. Just invisible tracts in the air, leftover from the thermal mining of the atmosphere.

Yeah, the conquistadors got the air too. Little known fact. When they'd first arrived, everywhere they looked they saw veins of silver in the ground. But when they'd drained the mountains dry of ore, they vacuumed the air of silver dust as well—using crude hand pumps that left an irresolution of pressure, forming the sky veins that have been there ever since. People learned to walk holding their children, papers, picking tools tight. Learned to expect and endure the inevitable whoosh when they blundered through one, that sick feeling in your stomach like an elevator dropping, when the air pressure shifts around you, the ground falling away for a moment while your feet dance just a hair above the earth.

Legend has it that the sky veins run all the way into orbit. Maybe beyond.

"I KNOW there is a God," says Nastasia, my picking partner.

That's not a real thing, picking partner, but we found each other in these heaps, and we like picking in each other's company better than we like picking alone. Although we don't talk much, and we don't ever spend time together after, or before. So, technically I'm still pretty close to alone. But we do pick alongside each other, and that's something.

"I know there is a God," Nastasia says to herself—but also, because I am there, to me—at the outset of each day of picking. "The metal breeds like a sow."

She tries to make us feel optimistic about the haul. I must have that despairing look in my eyes all the time now, the one I used to hide with sunglasses. But I lost my glasses somewhere in my rented warren above the butcher shop back in town, or in the streets, or at the noodle stall. And now my feelings are just out there, splashed all over my face for everyone to see. My eyes are bigger and more expressive than a man's eyes ideally should be. With long dark lashes. There's not a woman who's studied my face who hasn't voiced jealousy. But they're soulful. I hate it.

If you archived every one of the not-so-many pictures ever taken of me you'd see me squinting as if into the sun. Even when there is no sun. Narrowing my eyes, hiding their brown depths. Except the pictures with you in them. Then I'm laughing, my face crinkled up like a rotten red apple in that way you used to sweetly poke fun of, then crawl up on my chest to plant little kisses on my (rotten red apple) cheeks. So, really, my eyes are narrowed in those photos too, but from smiling.

Anyway, Nastasia's only sort of right. Every day the metal spills further out into the road, and the mess is greater, wilder. But it's not that there's more of it, just that it spreads. Rats root in it, knocking around with a sporadic clanging that shakes me awake every night. Packs of kids kick through it in the day. Loud herds of kids that remind me of you. Spots of speed in the throbbing sunshine.

NASTASIA AND I get along because we're picking for opposite things. She's hunting for discarded silver. There's hardly any about, but she's determined, and has found a pinch or two over the past months. She carries a vial of liquid mercury and a leather pouch of salt. She hunches down, fizzling salt over the scraps, then douses them with a drop of mercury. She grinds at the metal with an iron spoon, looking for the telltale darkening as the salt and mercury decompose into a slurry, expressing some hidden grain of silver.

I grab at any large scraps of tin. I'm not picky, just looking for the big ones. Then I lash them together with straps and lug them on my shredded, bleeding back, my denim shirt crunchy with dried brown streaks. I pick up the big slabs, and Nastasia pokes around underneath for any sequestered silver. From the outside, I suppose we look like one of those typical pairs of strays, a big dog and a small runty one that's seemingly leeched on for protection. I always saw these duos and wondered why the big guy doesn't want another big friend. But the truth is, Nastasia tires less easily than I do. More than once she's brought me a cold amberade with crushed ice from one of the street vendors while I sit collapsed on a pile of tin, wilting in the sun like a lady at a garden party.

And I like the sound of her nearby. I like her permanent hunch, and the vaguely sour scent that her thin old skirts give off. Reminds me of my mother, I guess. So long gone now in the cold city night, soot blowing in the windows as her soul blew out.

NASTASIA ASKED ME once about Pebble. He was the only thing of ours I had taken with me. After all, you said you didn't want him anymore. You'd outgrown him, I guess. Or it was too painful.

So I took him. The truth was, I couldn't bear to be without your stuffie. There, I said it. I needed Pebble. I talked to him at night, conjuring you, the way you used to ventriloquize his voice—that fake British accent you'd get, the pomp and circumstance that would get me bent over, gut-giggling in bed with you. I'd watch old movies on my pocketscreen with him—or, well, I tried to watch those difficult art movies you like. I'd prop Pebble up on a pillow next to me, but I couldn't get through much without you there, lying on my chest, explaining to me what in god's name is interesting about fifteen unedited minutes of cows mooing their way through a muddy village. A "long take," you'd once said it was. Something about the "de-reconciliation" (I think you made that word up) of everyday life and history. The cows' walking representing everyday life. History, I guess, being outside the frame.

But the ad spots kept interrupting and I'd get off on a tangent, reminding myself I needed to buy deodorant or work on my amalgams in the yard. It wasn't the same as watching with you, afterward singing our made-up national anthems for territories of no nation, falling asleep together holding hands. I felt safe knowing I was keeping you safe. I always told you Daddies miss their little girls worse than their girls miss them. It's true, Baby. Isn't it.

Nastasia only asked about Pebble once. I thought she'd seen him before then—this one particular day really early on, when we'd started running into each other in Potosí, but hadn't yet acknowledged to each other that we were intentionally walking together. In those days I'd walk just a bit behind her, or she'd walk just a bit behind me. Not meaning to, per se, but then again never losing sight of each other, somehow perfectly paced despite our gulf of size and age (neither of us young, but she's easily twice my nigh-on-middle-agedness, and probably half my wiry mass).

This was another one of those days when I got tired out and had to rest, and Nastasia had gone off to get me an amberade, then continued on her patient picking, quietly, like a chickadee hunting seeds amongst garbage, not too far off, but far enough away that I felt safe taking Pebble out. And Nastasia peeked over a couple times to see if I was ok. But she didn't see Pebble that day. Or if she did, she didn't say anything.

I took him out to feed him his amber, which was usually something I only did in absolute privacy. See, the people here know something about amber—same way they did back in the sixteenth century. Hell, actually, all the way back to Greek and Roman times, when amber was *hlector*, bestower of a healing magnetism. There is no question that they would think I was wasting it.

Nastasia had explained that you were supposed to swallow the amber grains at the bottom of the drink. She wasn't even from Potosí, but she paid attention, made friends, had even joined a Mahjong circle that met in the back of the bakery on Wednesday nights. Which is where she gathered most of her information. While picking, Nastasia would mix the latest Mahjong gossip—who'd been expelled, who reinvited, what rival circles had sprung up—with critical local knowledge.

In Potosí, she said, amber is a prized remedy meant to draw all the toxic elements out of the colon, so you'd excrete any excess mercury your body held, or piss it away.

"Health drink," Nastasia would say, pressing an amberade into my palm.

I'd glug it. Make grateful eyes at her, lifting my sunglasses over my brow to nod and give that little half-smile I could really not manage in my emotional state but did anyway. Then I'd filter the cold pine-rich water through my teeth, reserving the amber grains, sucking them clean. I'd spit them into my palm when Nastasia wasn't looking and push them into that little hole I made in Pebble's back.

At night, in the single room I'd rented above the butcher, with the scent of blood and Clorox spilling in the windows, I'd hold him close to my chest. Full of amber, he'd have gathered enough static in my pocket all day so that he'd be vibrating with electrical charge. I'd hold him to my chest and pretend he was you. Breathing against me. I'd feel his warmth.

THE AMBER is probably what caused it, but really it was my own un-thinkingness. I was out picking—it wasn't long after I got here, having taken the IndentureShip south to the Potosí mines looking for any kind of work I could get. It was just after I realized I could mix mercury amalgams with the tin to make my mirrors for skywriting. I figured if I could hit the Chinese moon lander's probe—Yutu 7—on its next cycle, I could flash you our made-up Morse code for "I Love You." Three taps forward, three back. Silent beat. Three forward and back again. Would you see it? I liked to believe you would. But what were the chances.

Anyway, I was out picking, and I was struck down with one of those hot shots of missing you. The ones I get hundreds of times a day. Memory-pain. And I was already in so much pain, with my back aching, and the blazing sun, sweat pouring in foul rivulets down the inside of my filthy old denim shirt.

And then I was remembering, and I wasn't there in the sun with Nastasia—not really. I was back in the night before our first Halloween.

JESUS YOU WERE PRECISE about pumpkin carving. I'm not a precise person. But you were. Insisted we needed to stencil the designs before cutting them. So you stenciled, and I selected designs. Happy, unthreatening pumpkins. A chill Halloween scenario. You probably would've chosen something weirder.

Rosenberg

You stood behind me tsking at every little falter I made with my knife. I told you to go sit down and be quiet, Daddy was working.

I gave you a catalog to choose any dress-up outfit you wanted. I said we could go to the store the next day and get whatever you liked. You said let's each write down what we like and compare notes. You wanted to see what I picked out for you to wear, what I wanted to see my darling daughter in.

When I finished with the pumpkins, and we lit them and carried them out to the pitch-dark patio where no one ever came anyway (we were so secluded there at the end of the cul-de-sac), we came back inside and wrote down our choices and exchanged them.

Slutty schoolgirl, yours said.

Little lamb outfit was mine.

Your upper lip curled in a combo smile and sneer. "You don't want slutty schoolgirl? Exactly how fucking young do you want me?"

You knew you had me. It was the Age of the Ultra Families, after all. Really, how could I escape this particular fantasy.

You wriggled your bare thighs around on that scratchy grey couch.

"Little lamb outfit with that burgundy G-string underneath," I confessed.

So that's what I was thinking of the day I lost Pebble.

And it's only burned on my memory that I was thinking of that, because of what came after.

I WAS WALKING along the streets with Nastasia, and I got that nauseous shot to my gut that meant some part of me—some unconscious part I was currently doing my best to stamp into submission—was remembering you. It stopped me in my tracks and I had to gasp for breath, the leather of my tin-straps cutting into my back with each sentimental wheeze. I was standing on one of the piles of tin, struggling for air, remembering: you wriggling on the couch, winking your legs open at me, my groin flaming hot and then I was between your legs, ripping your G-string off, and I was inside you.

Sometimes when we fucked—and that Halloween, if I remember properly, was one of those times—just to really turn me on, you'd hold Pebble's paw. *Ooh Daddy.* I'd look up—remove my head from the hot nook of your neck—and you'd be holding Pebble's little teddy bear fist in your own.

Goddamn it just threw me over the edge. You knew it would.

And so that day, there I was standing still on the pile of tin, gazing at Pebble, holding his paw, remembering you holding it, and—well, Baby, you might not know this but it is possible to hold back a single set of tears for several years straight. Many a filmic crescendo—not in those art movies you watch, but the schlock your Daddy watches—having to do with masculinity confirms this fact. Quiet shot of car interior. Night driving. Aging guy (red rotten apple face, say). Hands on wheel. Beard scruff. Black night. Cue music. Here it comes.

Wet eyes.

So, yeah, I was holding Pebble's paw and fucking crying. Or, well, tearing up at least.

Nastasia must've heard something and looked over.

She didn't look too alarmed, but she did ask, "You bring toys with you to pick?"

And I croaked out, "My daughter's."

Not exactly the truth, but close enough.

I DIDN'T KNOW a daughter was what I was looking for until I found you. On our first date, you spent the entire evening grilling me about world history, current affairs, and the hidden political stakes of seemingly innocuous legislation. It was clear that you were in possession of the answers, whereas I had fumbled my way into a decent but inglorious position as a minor bureaucrat at the Ministry of Financial Affairs. A job that I would soon lose, as it turned out, anyway.

It was a night of being endlessly harangued by a beautiful woman. Not unpleasant but a bit exhausting. And then you asked me if I wanted children. I shrugged, but it was a shrug of: *Kind of, yes*. Which you had opinions about too. Something to do with how all of our hopes and dreams for futurity had been funneled into the project of children.

"It's so narcissistic," you said, "all these mini reproductions of the self." You stabbed a penne and sat back, waving it around to emphasize your point. "It's weird how we're only supposed to love little versions of ourselves. So privatized."

You hated privatization. This much was obvious from the answers on your dating profile, not to mention your useless graduate degree in Decolonial Commune Studies—a field that was being phased out from under your feet. You had little chance of getting a job in this area when they were closing departments right and left. A fact which, for some reason, you didn't seem concerned about. Although you'd been clear you didn't have a trust fund.

"Well, it's the Age of Ultra Families," I shrugged (again).

"Fuck the Ultra Families," you whispered, leaning forward and looking me straight in the eye. "I'm talking about the future of all of us," you gestured with your fork at the entire—sparsely populated, down-at-the-heels—restaurant as a microcosm of the world. "Not just some private family unit."

I realized then you were offering me something bigger than you, me, and a kid. You were offering me a way of caring about the well-being of, for lack of a better word, humanity. Instead of helicoptering over one particular small individual—making it your life's purpose to ensure that this one tiny person doesn't come into contact with poisoned water, ultraviolet light, vehicle exhaust, or even a flicker of boredom—we could devote ourselves to the precarious future of planetary life more broadly. Sure, there wouldn't be anyone to take care of us in our old age, but we weren't living toward a comfortable retirement, were we? We were engaging in the kind of selflessness that required fanaticism and gave, in return, a sense of purpose and meaning. And also, admittedly, the very real risk of arrest or expulsion in the Age of the Ultra Families. Which perhaps accounted for why you'd suggested we meet at Villa Papyri Lounge for our first date, a restaurant I was quite sure had been closed for decades, vines growing over its grey shingled face in that inauspicious bend on Route 17. It wasn't closed. But it wasn't exactly open, let's just say, either.

I realized then that the other people eating in the restaurant were, by and large, also leaning forward, whispering conspiratorially to their dining partners. This, I realized, was a recruitment station for— whatever you were.

WHAT YOU WERE was a rebel. A more glamorous term, really, than what it was. You ran a reading group out of the back of the Villa Papyri that met twice monthly. You invited me to attend. You hinted that, if I were interested, you could give me the passcodes to articles printed on vanishpaper, web addresses for songs that were broadcast on banned vanishchannels. You used terms such as *revolutionaries*.

Comrades. And, most illegally of all: *lovers*. Unmarried, unchildrened people who fuck each other without the explicit goal of marrying or childrening.

Well, I was sunk. I'd been trying to imagine myself a parent and here I was being offered a partner. It was appealing. In a sparkly, illegal kind of way. We were back at my place by then. I was getting kind of drunk off Old Grand-Dad bourbon. "Fuck the Age of the Ultra Families," I blurt-echoed.

"And still," you winked. "No one escapes their historical context."

Whatever that meant.

I wasn't in a place to inquire further at the moment. Because you were sitting on that old desk of my grandmother's—the only thing she left me, and my only inheritance in the whole world. Your ass was on my inheritance. It was perfect.

Time got extremely slow. You were wearing that dress that buttoned down the front. It had a small pull in the fabric up near the waist— I remember that—and fishnet stockings (long since out of fashion but what did it matter, dear god you looked good in them). Your eyes were bright and dark. I looked at you for some time.

You opened your legs a bit, twitched them open, really. Pursed your lips and smiled almost sarcastically. Watching you, I caught my breath, audibly, and you noticed.

"Oh my god," you said, "you're such a lesbian."

You didn't mean it cruelly. And you said it gently, because you knew something I thought I was hiding very well. That I had been a woman. And this meant—in your complex lexicon of desire and permission —that I could touch you.

No, you didn't mean it cruelly. Because you saw something about the quality of my desire: that I could feel you just looking at you. And that this was something of what it meant to be—or to have been, before my tits became the property of the California Municipal Waste Department—a lesbian. That a woman moving in your line of sight could have an effect that was total, atmospheric. That you could be hesitant, incapable, and not particularly interested in establishing the difference between touching and seeing. That you would indulge a dead love, dead in the eyes of the world, and valueless. A love that choked and burdened the mind, that might even be the very foundation of melancholy and despair. But, oh my long-lost love, looking at a woman you really get a feel for the way that fire is a phenomenon of touch. And my point is, if you have ever been a lesbian, you will not even have to touch a woman to know that.

But I did touch you.

I pushed up your skirt, and knelt between your legs.

And when I touched you, the years fell off you like feathers from a bluebird at molting time.

I was making my way up your body with my lips. Your body seemed stratified by scent zones. I began—as I could not help but begin—with that immediately enslaving draught between your legs (wet forest flowers/plum/salt). Out along the powdery broken-straw aroma of your inner thighs, the alkaline tide of your genitals transitioned into an only seemingly contradictory vinegary cream toward your waist. All remaining sourness flushed out by the time I arrived at your neck— a dry, bright scent. Rosewater and cut grass.

You were young by the time I reached your lips. Or, you acted young. You inhabited your body, suddenly, as a much younger girl than I had begun with. You let me see you in all your historicity—all your ages at once. Maybe this is just what it is to fuck in general. Though this didn't feel *in general* to me.

We fucked once on my grandmother's desk, and then again in my bed. Afterward, lying together in the boiling pockets of my snarled

Rosenberg

comforter, we tried to sleep. You were tossing and turning, and then before I knew it I was on top of you again. This time, growling in your ear, *Didn't I tell you to go to bed now, didn't I tell you to go to bed.* And you were whimpering and writhing and you said, your nose against my neck, *I'm sorry Daddy I'm sorry.* And we fucked again, and this time it was the fuck you can never get away from.

"CAN I CALL YOU THAT—Daddy?" you said the next night, over steaks at the Villa Papyri.

I reached across the table to cut your meat for you, by way of answer.

BECAUSE THE TRUTH was I wanted it too. That *kind of, yes* shrug I'd given when you asked if I wanted children—well, loving you had answered that, didn't it. I'd cut the crusts off your bread. Watch anxiously from the window when you went out to get the mail at the curb. Hold your hand when we crossed the street. No spinning the roulette wheel with child-rearing and having to end up spending all this time with what turns out to be an awful brat. I had the most beautiful, brilliant, sexy brat of a daughter I could have hoped for.

Still, everything ends. It was criminal, after all, not to be a reproductive unit in the Age of the Ultra Families.

"WHO DO YOU EXPECT to consume all the products we're producing if you don't make new consumers!" a blond, anger-ruddied bureaucrat screamed at us repeatedly the night they raided the Villa Papyri. He wore the silver pendant of the House of Cortés, legendary slayer of the Aztec Empire. An agent of the Ultra Families. Figured. This guy had drank so much of the Kool-Aid he had Kool-Aid coming out his eyeballs. He glowered at our vanishpaper (glitching, unfortunately, and not vanishing quickly enough), did a sarcastic, hateful reading of that evening's discussion topic: "Not Everyone on the Cul-de-Sac Needs Their Own Snowblower." After the reading—delivered at full volume and peppered by frequent expostulations about its wrongness while slapping his palm to his forehead—he shrieked, "No, the entire cul-de-sac cannot 'make do' with sharing one snowblower! First of all, how humiliating for the cul-de-sac! Second of all, good luck not being a self-contained family unit when the shortages hit which believe me they will! Food and commodity riots! What will you do then without your own snowblower!"

None of this was delivered as a question.

The rest of the reading group was silent, scuffing their feet. Their bravado was gone. But you were there, and things were already going wrong by that time between us anyway, no thanks to me. Or maybe I was determined to be some kind of idiot-hero.

"Fuck the Ultra Families," I spat at him.

SO HERE I AM in Potosí.

And there I was, that day, croaking out to Nastasia, "My daughter's," standing stock-still on that pile of shitty tin holding Pebble's paw in mine, and a tear wells up in my eye—probably the first tear in years—and I can't rub it away with my hand because it's got mercury and tin and sulfur oxides all over it, black with soot and poisons, and so I raise my right sleeve up to my right eye, and with my left hand, I go to fucking dab at my eye with the cuff, and I'm holding Pebble with my thumb and forefinger in my left hand, and I'm trying to use the middle finger of that same hand to work this dabbing action, and, Baby, why didn't I just stuff him back into the cargo pocket of my pants. Why didn't I just fucking put him back in my fucking pocket. Because I must have shifted and suddenly I'm in one of the sky veins. I'd crossed many of them before, but this one was different. And what with all the crying and the dabbing—I just—well, oh, there's no easy way to say this: there was a whoosh and Pebble flew out of my fingers and up into the vein.

It must have been the amber reacting to the ionic charge. It must have been that, not that I wasn't holding tightly enough. The fucking vein, the ones Nastasia was always warning me about, worrying over me, telling me to clip my ID papers to the inside pocket of my pants, in case the gust takes them. "Hard to get things back once you lose them," she'd warned. She meant the papers, but hell, she'd encountered my eye-soulfulness and everything, so who knows what she meant. And I'd shushed her for weeks, months maybe. I'd never run into a sky vein that was all that strong.

But as I stood there on the tin, watching Pebble bobble up and away into the vacuum the conquistadors had left behind so long ago— so quickly and irretrievably out of my poisonous filthy hands, so quickly now a property of the sky, a red speck hurtling up toward the perimeter of blue, the horizon and then the endless distance of space—I knew that she was right.

Memoirs of an Imaginary Country

Maria Dahvana Headley

THE CENTER OF THE EARTH is full of things the surface thinks it has discarded.

You called the year your explorers arrived in my country year 1. We called that year 10,077. You called us Utopians. We called you something else.

Every woman, I learned, later in my life than I should have, is someone's imaginary kingdom.

All explorers, I also learned, are liars when it comes to the truth of what they've touched. If you're the gap in the map, you know this much is true.

I was the kind of girl who would always be a child, you said. I should take pleasure in the simple things, and I should not learn to read or write. Too much knowledge, you told me, would destroy my sense of wonder. I dusted your books. I looked at the margins of the maps, the places marked with monsters.

When I met you, I was thirteen, and I already knew I was too ugly to be loved. I was strong, and I was smart, but no girl was allowed to have everything. My sister was pretty, which meant that she also had to pretend to be weak. Together, we did all the work girls do, unnoticed. She listened to you. I scrubbed. She smiled at you. I plotted our course. We were invisible in different ways. My face and her mind, my teeth and her claws. You approved of us. We were your household. You could not see the fire at our edges. We were your girls.

I'm ahead of myself. Time works differently where I'm from. Our history is written in books that go backward as well as forward. Our time is measured in birds flying down through volcanoes, octopi contracting through cracks in our sky.

I hold my homeland inside my head. Burned books and misplaced ones, moth-eaten, mildewed.

A short accounting of expeditions into my country, and places like it, from the beginning of time to now: in come the white men, dressed in helmets protecting their soft skulls. They hold their cameras like guns, their guns like cameras, their cocks like fine teacups. Click, click, two clicks, maps moldy, zippers rusting. Men pissing from the flies of their chinos. Why are they called chinos? Because the fabric was made in China by girls like me. What were chinos originally? Pants worn by soldiers who killed girls like me. Call them also khakis, the Urdu word for "dust." Call those soldiers white men who began their battles dressed in red, and shifted themselves into uniforms that better mimicked the terrain and the color of the people they were bloodletting.

Packets of sugar and caffeine in the explorers' hands, all of that harvested by simple, innocent, go-lucky girls like me. They pick their way through the jungle or through the forest, lucking past our traps, shitting in our streets and wailing for assistance. In come the white men, dressed in suits that crumple, walking across the bottom of the ocean and over deserts filled with bones. They burst from their vehicles like sentient pus, and begin to dig for youth, oil, magic, buried treasure. These things are all things the world has promised them. They adventure, claim, and conquer. The mission of white men is to denature nature.

I was taught by men like these men. Look at how you civilized me.

It is 1785, and you are writing a book about two siblings who fall into the center of the earth and there discover a race of rainbow-colored citizens eighteen inches tall, in a place that is otherwise much like Venice. You're translating as you go, into French from your native Italian, to make the contents more delicious, and also to avoid trouble in your own country.

Everyone is androgynous, happy and innocent, full of wonder and potential, in this Utopia populated by sun-worshipping nudists. Everyone suckles at everyone else's breasts, and all in all it's a lovely and sustainable situation. It's unusually peaceful. No one fights over jealousies. Everyone mates for life, and if other lovers are taken, it is done pleasantly. Children are hatched. Rules are obeyed. The people are a rainbow, but only the red ones have power. The rest are servants. They love being servants.

Your book is called *Icosameron, or, the Story of Edward and Elisabeth, Who Spent Eighty-One Years in the Land of the Megamicres, Original Inhabitants of Protocosmos, in the Interior of Our Globe*. A utopian narrative, written in French by Giacomo Casanova, a Venetian, published in Prague, 1787. Seventeen hundred pages long, and full to the margins with falsehoods. Bound in leather, nicely printed, complete with chapters on philosophy, theology, sexuality. Analysis of a noble though flawed culture untouched by the West. Birdsong sung by its citizens. Bravery done by its narrator. By the end of the book, the descendants of the two original explorers number twenty thousand sets of twins. They have taken over the hollow Utopia and taught its citizens about gunpowder, imaginary cars, firearms, fidelity, starvation—

Headley

You sold only a handful of copies. Readers lifted it and put it down again, wrinkling their noses as you looked on, Italian eagerness translated to French fury.

After all that, it was time to fill the bedchamber at the center of the Earth with your own glorious godly self, an autobiography of a brave man, exploring.

In some versions of your stories, Giacomo Casanova, I was your first love, and my name was Bettina. I met you when I was thirteen, a girl living in a house in Padua that took you in. You were a boy younger than I, and you fell through the ceiling of my life, and into the center of my family. I was forced into an exorcism to avoid your accusations of impropriety, into convulsions to prove my purity. All of this, you wrote, occurred because I was a vixen. I was married eventually to a shoemaker who beat me, and many years later, you sat at my deathbed and admired my ancient ugliness, wondering at how you yourself were still so vigorous and handsome. What wonderful memories you had of me, the curve of my hip as I pressed past you in a narrow hall, the way you could, at any moment, ask for breakfast and be fed everything I had.

In other versions, your name was Edward and I was your younger sister Elisabeth, birthing forty sets of twins for you in this country where tiny people worshipped a central sun, obeyed a pope, and sang instead of speaking. All of the residents of your Utopia had breasts, including me. You were the only one without. We took turns breastfeeding you so you wouldn't starve. Some of us died because of your appetite. We were all tremendously interested in your penis. We called you a giant.

Later, when we returned to the surface, I stood beside you while you explained why you'd married me. I had nothing to say about it, besides the occasional supportive murmur: "it only made sense." We'd fallen through the sea floor together, and you were my older brother, and we were two humans surrounded by noble innocents. We returned with stories of how we civilized them into submission, and the rest of our story, that of siblings marrying and populating a world that was already populated, fell aside. We were fertile and generous with our opinions. We were explorers. We were making the world better.

Sometimes in your accounts, you revised me again. I was, in those stories, not human, but a yellow girl from that city in the center of the Earth. I was all over your cartography: at once the X-marked diamonds and gold, and the sectors etched with monsters. I was a discovery, newly set in moveable type, printed in Prague, and invented into a wilderness worthy of an audience. That is the closest version, if there's a truth between your lines.

I am well aware of the world. The outside is a place that was once covered in green, and now the green places are brown. The reefs are quiet. The caves that held sleeping bears now contain only skeletons. People like you still live unsheltered, on the roof. Is it not obvious who is civilized?

There is a skillful hand-colored etching of you at the front of your book. You're wearing expedition attire, though in your version this is a factual manuscript discovered in a library, a twenty-night tale of adventures had by someone other than you. In the illustration, you are rakish, periwigged, a loose brush rendering your face more handsome than it might have been in life, but who would judge that? You were, of course, the foremost expert on your own actions. No one other than another white man could possibly understand your mind.

This was your country.

You revised me repeatedly: a girl from a realm reachable only by fateful accident, her topography penciled, her thoughts pinned to paper like ethered insects. Your surveyors missed my volcanoes but found my caves. They filled them up to keep themselves from falling in.

MY SISTER AND I were looking up when the invaders fell out of the sky, into the center of one of our cities. Elisabeth arrived with sunken cheeks and wild eyes, and Edward with scurvy. The two of them had been traveling by ship to the North Pole. They were not without wealth, though they were in dire straits due to being caught in an embrace mid-voyage. They bribed another ship and, bent on escape, hid in a casket of resplendent clothing. They paid a sailor to throw them overboard, but they missed the raft and sank. They plummeted through a crevasse, dropping through our roof and into a river.

They were too heavy to float, and so they descended like wriggling rocks. From our observation point, we could see their thighs, worm pale, piss-ribboned. It was clear they were frightened of us. He had a knife and she had a rock, and they held their weapons tightly.

"More of them," said my grandfather. "I thought we'd closed the hole. It's been years."

"Blame the stitcher," said my grandmother, and went into the house.

Some of us were small, and therefore interested.

"They're like animals," said my mother, but we could hear the uncertainty in her voice. The last group had come in when she was only ten, and she hardly remembered them.

"Pets?" said my sister, her hand cupped to stroke. "Or meat?"

"No," said my mother. "They bite. Keep your fingers to yourself."

As we watched, they interlaced their own hands and nodded furiously, looking at us as though we might carry their bags in from out of the rain.

"We are explorers!" shouted the man.

"*Brave* explorers," she whispered to him. "From the higher place!"

The children crept into their trunk to leaf through possessions as the explorers marched through our streets, planting flags with their faces drawn on the fabric.

"This is our country," she said, and then looked at him. "It was made for us. No one will make us leave. Look at them. They can't even speak. They're awestruck."

She wiggled her fingers as one might wiggle fingers at a puppy.

The children were standing in a circle watching the pests. We'd been set to keep them from moving through town.

My sister held out her hand, though, and the man looked at her. She was beautiful, my sister, and she offered him a piece of bread. She could not help her kindness. My sister fed the starving, and these two were so stupid, so drenched, she assumed they were hungry.

"This is our country," the man agreed, taking the bread and biting into it with teeth that were, yes, pointed. "These are our subjects. We'll be the king and queen," he said, looking around, his eyes bright. "They need parents. It's our duty."

"*Sacred* duty," said the woman. "How will they know the rules, if we don't rule them?"

I didn't know their stories about the center of the Earth. One of them was that it would be an Eden, a place into which a man might tunnel, and take everything he ever wanted away with him when he went, all of it tucked into a kicking, shrieking sack and transported to Venice.

The words the people outside used for those actions included: *forage, harvest, teach, discover, explore, civilize.*

There were other words, if you ask me, and if you ask my sister.

"Oh!" said the woman from outside to her brother. "What a relief, Edward, to be free of the constraints of society! Oh, what joy to be amongst these dear little nobodies!"

Headley

"Oh!" said the man from outside to his sister. "What a haven we've discovered, Elisabeth, what a perfection!"

"They needed us," she said.

"They prayed for us," he replied.

"And we descended," they said in unison.

IT'S 1790, and Giacomo Casanova's utopian novel has failed utterly. No one understands him. He is disconsolate, lamenting, locked in a room full of books, feeding on crusts and the occasional feast by librarians and patrons. He is tragic.

A young woman sends him a letter inspiring him to write his sexual history, at length and in detail. *Well, then*, he thinks, and begins a flattering account, humorous, wry, brazen, flirtatious.

Venice. Through it walks a brilliant young man who is sometimes a scholar and sometimes a gambler, and often nothing but a sprinting seat in sheepskin pants, sighted from a window as he leaps into the bush, pursued by hundreds, literally hundreds, of husbands. He is heroic.

He descends a rope made of bedsheets and clambers into a bathtub, the daughter of the house assigned to soaping him. She has never known a man before. Not that he is a man. He's twelve. She's thirteen. She has never heard of sin, and her body is a creation made of velvet and silk floss combined with just a little bit of cow, and she will let you have anything—truly anything—your heart desires. She is Utopia. Climb inside.

Paradise, he writes, is a girl on her back, her legs open, and inside her a mystery. If she were to be sliced down the center, civilization would pour out, the men of Earth, thumbkins, each one with a tiny voice and all of the reason found in the libraries of the ancient world. Men are born with reason. Women are windowless wombs, and they must be taught the rules. They are ribs and fibs, broken and expendable. They are lies meant for laying. That is not to say they aren't wonderful. Some of them are witty. Others are wicked. Others are ugly but strangely skillful in the bedchamber, and who would imagine that?

He goes on this way for a while.

No, he revises the story. There are two girls. There are four. Oh! The glory! There are ten, and all of them bend to admire him, everyone in the story living in perfection, everyone astonished, joyful and terribly lucky.

I WAS THE KIND OF GIRL who was born to do work, while the other kind was born for breeding, the people from outside told me. Those were the rules of civilized places, places such as the one they came from. While my sister was in the upstairs room in labor with her first set of twins, I boiled water and scrubbed a floor. This was how everything gleamed, how everything worked the way it should. Rules brought by rulers to the ooh-ahh innocents of elsewhere.

The two explorers were naked in bed, by then, breakfasting on pastries I'd baked. The woman from outside had stood over me in the kitchen, instructing me on the finer points of dough. "I suppose you're used to raw meat," she whispered to me, and giggled, holding my hand.

Elisabeth had hair of no particular color, and a mouth full of bad teeth. She thought she'd brought fire to the inside, never noticing our chimneys spitting smoke. She herself liked to smoke a pipe carved in the shape of her own former face, which ten years into her time here had significantly expanded.

Edward was a man with a mouth that never stopped moving. He gave us names and counted us, though we already had names and families. He made a book of our history, which he did not know. He claimed he could see our thoughts by looking at us. He was a gun-bearing tooth of a tiger, and we did not like his look. We did not wish him to take us to the city. Some days he had notions of ships and chains and fireworks, and on other days he declared that he would pour us into tiny blown-glass bottles and use our sweat to scent the pale throats of the finest ladies of Venice.

"What a wonder," he said. "You know nothing of sin. You are sugar grown in darkness."

I looked up at the bright orb at the center of our sky.

"When the world was flat," he told my sister, "there were stories about the people who lived in the dark. You people. When it stormed on the surface, all the blind creatures came up to taste the rain, but when it was dry, back down again they went. When the world curved into a sphere, and the edges were no longer places from which to plummet, the stories swelled to fill the spaces. You're a story."

"The world," Elisabeth offered to me one morning, "is a cinnamon chocolate with a crispy shell, and an interior of cherry in syrup. The world is a black rubber ball wrapped in kid leather. The world is a snail, the shell a house and inside the shell, a sentient softness, pliant as a woman's flesh. Watch as it uncurls, watch as it looks up in wonder at the man who has at last plumbed it."

She stretched on her back, asking for a massage. "Do work out the knots," she said. I considered a rope I'd tied about my waist.

"This is perfection," said Elisabeth.

"*We* are perfection," said Edward, and he took her hand in his, and with his other hand he touched my sister's waist, and wiped butter onto her skirt.

YOU WERE ALWAYS writing about the same kind of kingdom, whether it was your memoir of lovers or your novel about a wonderful world within a rocky womb. Milk-fed masqueraders and a boy in the middle, an innocent himself, this intelligent explorer who brings guns and poisons, who eats of the forbidden trees, who fucks his way through the center of a civilization and is worshipped for it.

You dreamed your way into my country, and with you came the creatures of your skull, each one a beast of bones and calligraphy.

I dreamed my way into your country, and with me came my sister and my parents, my grandparents, our fingers and hands, our knives. I was the center of the Earth, and you were the one who tunneled into me.

We knew that the people above us were speakers and breathers, diggers and bearers. We weren't blind. We weren't thirsty. We never rose up through the mud. Was our city made of glory? It was not. It was a city like any city, buildings with worms in the grout, rotten tubers, unjust laws. It was ours.

Shall we speak of you? You told your own story, and you never stopped telling it. You believed that there was silence in our country before you, and that yours was the first voice to bring us knowledge.

You thought you taught us to talk, but we had been speaking. You thought you taught us to live, but we had buildings and music, fire, books, and paintings. We were nowhere, you said, when you appeared in our universe.

You thought I wasn't fit for fucking. I busied myself with other tasks. I learned your language. I learned your dreams. I came into the bathroom and soaped your back as you reclined, looking at the ceiling, writing a book about other women.

"You're so tiny," you told me, as though you were a giant. "Just look at you," you said tenderly. "Like a child."

Headley

What explorer has not longed to bring his guns to an undiscovered country, so that he might casually become king? In your bathtub, you crowned yourself, and looked at me, and raised your scepter. This was nothing new. I'd seen your kind before.

In the other version of your stories, the part you weren't writing down, you put my sister in a sack. I leapt in with her. We were kept in the darkness, thrown over your shoulder, smuggled out of paradise and into hell. We traveled, whispering to the surface, and when we arrived in your city, you opened the sack and smiled, because you'd brought us to a better place. Or, perhaps, you had made your own place better by taking us from ours.

In the version you wrote, my sister and I were one person, constituted entirely of love. We opened our shirt to feed you from our breasts, though we were ourselves starving. We were awed at the sight of your sun, dazzled at the wonder of your world. You grieved when you thought we might die, though this would make your own journey less complicated. You'd been thinking of where to put us: a zoo, a museum?

You dumped us onto the floor and went to your library. I went to the kitchen. My sister went to the bedroom. You could not see our edges. We were your girls. You didn't know our thoughts. You didn't know what was beneath the mattress. You didn't know what was in the pocket of my apron.

Time passed.

There are other versions of our stories, just as there are other versions of yours: in come the white men, and they get sick, which throws them on the mercy of the people they're invading. We are in the trees watching as they arrive on stretchers, snake-bitten, feverish, starving, fighting furiously with one another, Pilgrims, fur trappers, journalists and geographers, millionaires, filmmakers, translators who speak nothing near our language, preachers who say they'll teach us, teachers who say they'll reach us. *Untouched*, they say, and touch us.

Call death a kind of exploration. Call hands on someone else's skin a kind of expedition. Call us the ground, and call yourselves a flag.

And now see what we call you. You are the dragon we slay, the ship we wreck. Your safety is not our business.

This is not the story you wrote. This is the story we wrote.

I was the kind of girl who was born to serve, the people from outside told me, while I sharpened their knives. I was working in their kitchens. I was always mistaken for a cook, by you, by them, by everyone. I had the kind of face that looked kindly, the kind of body that looked built to enfold the hungry. I held a knife up to the firelight and tested the blade on my fingertip. It worked the way it should. I was no stranger to knives.

I had my sister with me, her twins nursing, and we were writing the battle plan, the two of us diagramming armor, inscribing knife hilts with names other than the ones they thought they'd given us. We could read and write. We had our own names, and our own language.

You thought you knew what we wanted, but we had wants of our own.

Here is something I learned in the hundreds of years I spent in the center of the Earth and later in the libraries and bedchambers, pressed between your pages, carving my way out of your stories with one of the knives you gave me to show your readers that I was a spitfire, a flame-breathing beauty with black hair and barbed bits.

Imaginary countries and imaginary cunts are in the same category. They are the same story.

Look at this volcano, the heat of the center of the Earth pouring out in flame. Look at the way the outside splits open and becomes the inside, the way that helmets are not enough to keep your soft skulls safe. Look at the catastrophe of birth.

My sister and I are coming up from beneath the ground, our fingers tipped in claws. We are springing through the soles of the feet of the men standing over our home. Your name is a synonym for swing, and my name

Headley

is earthquake, taking your library and opening its contents to the elements, tearing your chinos thread by thread into nests for the birds whose eggs you've broken. The center of the Earth is not a windowless room, but a room with a long view to the sky, not a hollow object, but a goblet full to spilling.

Call it a skull. Call me a demon. Call me a disastrous expedition, a haunted pilgrimage. Know that I am still drinking from your bones.

You are the book I am writing. You are the story I am searing into the skin of the ones who come after me. I name you after myself. I call your country after my sister. I plant a flag in your heart and drive it in, claim your territory and tell the world that no one was here before I arrived.

Are you an old man now? You are. Are you wordless, your hand shaking as you write your adventures? You break into convents. You break into caverns. You are the best worst they ever had.

Listen to me tell your story. You've lost the ability to speak. You're standing before all the men of your generation, trying to tell them that you've won, but your footage is forgotten. There is no one left for you to call to. You will have to call for me.

You think I'm the kind of girl who'd ask you to write the story of your life.

"Ti amo," you say to me. I have not been brought to the surface to feed you milk. I traveled with you not because of love, but because of fury. My sister mothered your children. Our sense of wonder was intact. We wondered at your frailty.

"Je t'aime," you try.

Am I the woman now, here at your crumpled bedside, holding a spoon? And here is my sister on the other side of the bed, holding a knife.

"Ich liebe dich," you whisper.

Look at how we are young and you are ancient.

"Open your mouth," I say to you, in a language you never learned. "Let me close your gaps. Let me fill you up."

"Let me imagine your future," says my sister.

Athena Dreams of a Hollow Body

JR Fenn

AFTER THE RECALL the apartment felt empty. No mother removing baklava from the oven to the ding of some internal timer. No mother beavering away on her computer. No mother wired into her battery pack at night, whirring and still in the flickering blue light of the charger.

I missed her. I missed her oil-and-plastic smell, the curved dome of her hair that was never out of place. I curled on the living room floor under her Charge-Pak casing, the hum of electricity soothing me to sleep. I missed her reassurances, the cool touch of her fingers to my forehead, her glances and small offerings of food when I'd had a bad day.

My roommate Sue was glad. "Thank God your mother's not here anymore!" she called from the bathroom as she slapped her avocado egg-yolk mask on her face. "There was something wrong with her!"

I wasn't sure about Sue by that point. Maybe it was the fact that she'd never really given my mother a chance, from the day the box arrived in the mail. "I don't like the way she looks at me," Sue had said as she pulled on her blue trench coat and looped her umbrella through the belt so it dangled by her side like a nightstick. She pushed her glasses up her nose and glared in the direction of the kitchen. My mother just stood in the doorway, her feather-duster attachment extended from her hand like a miniature palm tree. She smiled at Sue, a gentle smile that was hard to read. My mother did not talk much. "It's like living with a mime!" Sue said.

I liked having a mother, though, especially when nobody was around. We'd putter around the apartment, tidying or rearranging things or just working on our computers. My mother made progress on her own little projects, the clack of the keys intermittent and considered. When I took breaks from my online tutoring, it was nice to have a mother to chat with, especially in light of the bionuts who never failed to pop up on my discussion boards at Phalanx University. When I asked my mother what she thought of biomoms, she lifted her shirt and pressed an invisible button. A sliding panel opened to reveal an interior cavity sort of like a toaster oven. "COOK YOU!" she said in her loud, furry voice, the "C" words formed with difficulty, both index fingers pointing into her cavity—"BAKE CAKE!" A terrible joke about gestating me. We both knew the idea of my coming from inside her body was just a metaphor, a myth of connectedness, but that didn't matter, because her eyes seemed to brighten as she pointed into her torso's recess, and when I laughed she gave a mix of a bark and a chuckle back. After that I felt better about returning to the dismal posts on my screen.

"The Mystery of Our Origins" covered evolution, evolutionary psychology, the history of science, and modern reproductive technologies, though it was of course "lite" because everything at the behemoth profit-making Phalanx online degree mill was "lite." I had no expertise in the area other than the fact that I was a product of said technologies. It was through this class, to be fair, that I'd learned of the existence of the mothers and had decided to order one for myself. *Feel what it feels like to have a mother*, the banner ad popped up, probably in reaction to my

Googling "assisted reproduction" and "the death of the nuclear family" as I paged through the week's reading on my computer. *Your very own mother in your very own home.*

I could admit to my mother that one student in particular had gotten under my skin. TeenMom insisted on responding to every prompt with her random thoughts about the fact that she had given birth. *Describe Darwin's idea of the origin of species.* "I felt my baby kick inside me," she wrote, "and I felt the miracle of life." *Discuss Watson and Crick's contribution to modern science.* "I became a passage for a force greater than myself. My body opened and made way for a cosmic energy bigger than I was, bigger than the baby I brought into the world. I became a conduit for a universal power that lifted me up as it moved through me, a hollow body floating in ether."

I could not rid myself of this strange image. It troubled me, intruding into my consciousness when I least expected it. I started to dream that I had become this hollow body, my form suspended in a swath of stardust like the Milky Way, light coursing through me the way water pours through a vase without a bottom.

"What's up with you?" Sue peered at me from the doorway to my room. I turned from my desk and my mother turned from hers, each of us stationed in front of a window so we could sit in the natural light as we worked. The honks and voices of the street floated up from below, cushioned by panes of glass. Both of us stared at Sue in her thin plaid button-down with pearl snaps, her skinny jeans finished with flat boots, so tight and in control of herself, her hair clipped around her beautifully shaped head, her glasses pert and glittering.

Sue worked at a bookstore. The bleached paper smell she brought home lingered in the air after she'd passed through the common spaces. Sometimes she left her shirt hanging over the back of a chair at the kitchen table, and once her boyfriend Todd abandoned his shoes in front of the oven, two gutted canvas trainers with ties as white as his teeth when he forced his lips into a smile—this back when he still came over.

I'd kind of liked Sue when she responded to my ad on Netlist. She'd asked me what I liked to read and showed some interest in the old home decorating magazines I collected from thrift stores around the city, so I rented her the room. In the early days, we had a pretty good time. We'd meet in the kitchen at odd hours and exchange a few pleasantries. It was nice to have another human being just down the hall, a whole other life unfolding in the orbit of mine.

Once I got my mother, though, Sue made me self-conscious. There we'd be, my mother and I, having dinner together at the little table in front of the kitchen window. Sue would blow through the door with Todd, their faces wet from the rain, their raincoats dripping happy wet plops onto the floor under the coat rack as they disappeared into Sue's room, where they'd laugh in low voices. After a while Sue might appear to pour some of her expensive tequila into two glasses. "Enjoying a nice dinner together?" she'd say, and swoop off back to her bedroom. Her tone made it seem as though my mother and I were a pitiful sight, my mother's plate empty and gleaming and mine full of half-devoured eggplant parmesan, one of my mother's specialties, congealing in an underwhelming mass before me.

A siren blared from the hospital around the corner. "What's up with you?" Sue repeated from the doorway. She shot a worried look at my stained shirt. Beside me, my mother returned her attention to her keyboard.

"What?" I said. "Tutoring." And I turned back to see what Teen-Mom had posted in response to *Compare the evidence for the Big Bang to the evidence for creationism.*

"A baby floated inside my body for nine months and it changed me forever," she wrote. "Becoming a mother has allowed me to connect to the space inside each of us where our design first unfolded. I cannot see another person without witnessing them small and hairless and suspended in the fluid of their mother's womb. I cannot go outside because I'm overwhelmed by the nascence in the people around me, their once-smallness, the child faces peering out from deep within their grown ones. The fact that we are all in such a radically unfinished state, a state of such fierce becoming, squeezes me so tight I cannot breathe."

IN MY DREAMS, in the middle of my hollow body, a small life grows. It is the size of a light-prick, so bright it sends rays through the white-translucent layers of my human shape, suspended in space and the fog of stars.

When I told my mother part of me wanted a baby the bio way, inside my body, she closed her computer and pushed my hair back from my forehead, her skin as soft as real dermis. "YOU CAN," she said. "YOU CAN!" Her volume modulation was way off, and she could only speak in two-chunk segments, subject and verb. The month I placed the order I'd been tight on cash; I wished I hadn't dialed the speech aptitude down to the bare minimum. When I tried to talk to her about my disorienting cravings, all she could say was "MAKE BABY!" and "HAVE BABY!" These were her sole responses to my confused mutterings about pregnancy and my running commentaries on my Internet searches for "biobirth." She reached the height of invention with "PINCHY BABY!"—this paired with crab fingers in response to a Google image of a three-month-old with an abnormally large and adorably chubby head. I wondered if she truly believed what she was saying or if this stuff was some kind of preordained script implanted by the manufacturer.

Fenn

CHARACTERIZE THE CONTRIBUTIONS of Rosalind Franklin to DNA sequencing. "I feel myself expanded from the inside," TeenMom wrote. "Having a baby is like knocking through a wall to a room in your heart you never knew was there."

It was the middle of the night again, the city clamped down into lone wanderers and ambulance songs in the distance. My mother had plugged herself into her Charge-Pak and was humming with sleep in the corner of the living room. I'd fought my insomnia in the dark and then hiked to the kitchen table where I leafed through my magazines, scissors in hand. Nothing caught my eye, so I opened my laptop.

TeenMom had added a reply to her own post: "It is a huge room. It is a room where love busts through the walls like a flood of light."

I scrolled through the next day's readings on sociobiology. I was typing my prompt when Sue swanned in and opened the fridge to pour herself a glass of hibiscus tea she'd made in my fake crystal pitcher. Sue was spending more time at Todd's place, and when she was home her light stayed on until two or three in the morning as she worked her way through the piles of books she brought home from the store. She could read until her eyes fell out; she was curious that way. She drifted over to the table and rifled through my collection of cutouts, which I kept in an old cake tin. I didn't appreciate her fingers spidering through the tin, upsetting my clippings. She pulled out two pictures. In the first, a woman in a pink shirt cupped her hand over her belly, her face left out of the photograph except for a smiling mouth and chin in soft focus. In the second, a man and a woman stood inside their kitchen, his arms around her, leaning together over the roundness at her middle.

"You must be ovulating or something," Sue said. "Are you taking your protentials?"

I nodded, though I couldn't quite remember the last time I had. Protentials suppress ovulation and all the feelings that go with it, the biggest thing since the pill. I didn't like the taste of the drops, or the way their brown color spread through water and settled in a molasses residue at the bottom of the glass. They made me uncomfortable, a scratchy discomfort deep in my middle, as though the growth of some essential impulse had been arrested there.

Sue bent down to squint at another picture, a small blond child holding his hands up in a gesture of victory. "Propaganda," she said. She ran her finger over the boy's face. "Up your dose."

Of course Sue would say that. Like many women our age, she'd sworn off descendants. "What's the point," she'd said one morning as she poured her organic almond milk into a bowl, "in squandering the life of the mind? Reproduction," she shivered. "It's like a nightmare from the Dark Ages." She'd sipped the cream of the almond milk straight from the bowl, no cereal or anything, her body unsullied and compact.

Now she opened the freezer and dropped three ice cubes into her tea. "You may as well move to the hinterlands," she said, "where women still devote themselves to wiping noses, changing diapers. I couldn't even imagine it." She swept off back to her room, cubes clinking in the glass.

I wondered if I was having the urge to reproduce, if ordering a mother had been some kind of nesting instinct. I stared at the small child in the magazine picture and considered what it might be like to have a childhood. They had photographed his victory stance on a green lawn with a blurry house in the background. Someone had put flowers on the porch, smears of color; beyond one of the upstairs windows lay the boy's own bedroom. Somewhere inside that house lurked parents who did his laundry and read him books and tucked him in at night.

Like Zeus's daughter, I had stepped out of my maker fully grown. I remembered looking back at his face the instant after I emerged to see the empty windows of his eyes and the metal of his mouth—the door through which I had stumbled in my rush outward hanging open, twisted on its hinges. The air felt cold on my skin and the light of the world stung my eyes. My feet pressed down with a special kind of pain. I would soon learn the words for it: *flesh* and *floor* and *gravity*.

I'd come to this apartment fully grown, suitcase in hand; I'd gone to college and begun my work as an online pseudo-professor. At least one of my donors must have been advanced in the IQ category; unlike most, I could remember the cool green of the pod water, the tickle of the respirator bubbles tracing their way up my spine. I sometimes envisioned meeting them, an awkward roundtable where I blathered on to a circle of blank faces as I scoured their bodies for my features: a pear-shaped trunk here, an aquiline nose there, eyes the color of scorched earth staring back at me. But none of them ever surfaced, a common enough occurrence in assisted reproduction. Somewhere between donating and watching my naked body grow and grow in the pod, they'd changed their minds about wanting a connection.

I took my laptop into the living room where my mother's face had closed down, her eyes shut and her mouth curled in on itself as if she were dreaming of something nice to eat. I went to my room and sprawled on the softness of my bed to check the discussion board again. TeenMom had logged on and seen the new prompt but she hadn't posted. For some reason I started to worry. I wondered what she was doing, if her baby needed her, if he was wawling for her through the cold dark halls of her house. I felt a weird twinge of jealousy at his cries.

I clicked on the button to write a new message. The empty dialogue box stared at me, white and clean. I didn't know what to say, but I wanted to say something. I tried some variations. I deleted them. Finally I settled on two sentences: *I did not have a mother. But now I do.*

I clicked send.

After a while of waiting for a reply, I went to bed.

In the morning, a bright red flag indicated that I had an unread message.

"This is inappropriate sharing on the part of instructional staff," TeenMom said. "Please do not private message me with personal information again."

How did TeenMom get to be such a good writer, I wondered. It wasn't usual for Phalanx students. I posed my question in a message and pressed send.

"Most people think biomoms are sick in the head or something," TeenMom posted. Here she inserted a frowny face with angry wrinkles across the forehead. "Most people do not know that having a baby fills you with the joy and grief of an *exponentially increased clarity of mind*. All of a sudden you can see *every fucking thing in the world for what it is* like a stark and vivid slap in the face. You cannot fool yourself any longer; you do not lie to yourself as you did before. You become empty; you let your love for others course through you and clean you out completely until nothing is left."

A while later she added: "emptiness = beauty." After these words she inserted another emoticon, a surprise face with pink cheeks, round eyes, and a mouth in the wide shape of an O.

AS THE COURSE went into its final week there was less for me to do and I settled back into a domestic rhythm. I expected my mother to join me in all the little tasks we loved—simmering ginger, cleaning the baseboards with toothbrushes—but she was always off doing something else, keeping her own routine. It was around this point when I realized that as much as Sue did not like my mother, my mother also did not like Sue. I'd come upon my mother in the bathroom, her stiff bust silhouetted by the window, staring at Sue's toiletries. Once I even found her in Sue's room; there was something strange about the way she stood there gazing at Sue's neat, clean-smelling rows of clothes—something vacant and hostile.

"She has to go," Sue hissed one day, conscious of my mother nearby, and when the notice arrived I shoved it in the trash, but the phrases kept echoing in my head. *Model defective. Hazard to the public. Mandatory return to manufacturer subject to enforcement.* So when the box came I read the instructions. I went to where my mother sat at her desk, a miniature vase with a metal flower perched by her elbow. She worked away merrily, hitting one key and then another with her index fingers, pausing to hunch toward the screen with her face a few inches away, so wrapped up in her train of thought she didn't notice me come in. I put my hand on her shoulder and she looked up, grinned, and closed her laptop. I knelt and put my arms around her waist. She leaned her head against mine, the hum of her internal mechanism slow with calm.

I smelled the sweetness of silicon and magnets, a hint of the powder she dusted on her feet. And then my fingers found the switch, concealed under the plate that protected her spine. When I pressed it she turned to metal and parts, nothing more than an empty shape. When I picked her up she felt extremely light, her arm dangling like a loose sock, her chin tipped back and rolling on its joints. I laid her inside the box and closed the lid. Then I propped the box outside the apartment door for the postman. It depressed me to see it there in the hallway, so normal-looking it might have held anything.

Back in my room, my laptop screen glared at me, the discussion board frozen on TeenMom's last post. Next to me, my mother's chair sat unoccupied in the light. I wondered what she had been working on with so much concentration. I moved across to sit at her desk and opened her laptop.

The screen blinked into life, split by two panels. On the left, an Internet search for "LOVE DAUGHTER" displayed 283 million results. On the right, an icon hovered, a Word doc titled "ILOVEYOUATHENA." In all our conversations, my mother had never used a complete sentence. I wondered if her writing protocols had outstripped her speech programming. When I opened the doc, it filled the right-hand side of the screen in a perfect upright rectangle so I could still see the search results, just as my mother must have arranged the windows in order to go back and forth between the two.

The document was slow to load. It was huge—214 pages to be exact, as I could see when the count in the bottom bar stopped climbing. It was written in a variety of thick italic scripts, all in different fonts, as if they'd been copied and pasted and rearranged:

> *I love my daughter more than . . . i remember the first time she . . . **I laughed so hard I . . . ! I will never forget the smell of . . . , the way she . . . Watch this video.** That was our trip to . . . THAT WAS WHEN SHE FIRST . . . **She finally fell asleep on . . . ! My daughter makes me feel . . .** I love her more than . . . Remember the first time she . . . ? **CHECK THIS VIDEO!** This was when she first started . . . ! isn't she . . . ?!? **I want her to KNOW she is MORE . . . ! I NEVER KNEW** having a daughter would be so . . . !! **How could I have known this would be such . . . !?!?!***

And so on.

I scrolled through the text. It made me feel wobbly, the marshmallow glop of my soul jiggling in unbearable motions. I sprang to my feet and ran down the hall to fling open the door. The box was still there. I wrestled it back to my room and shoved it into the corner of the closet, my mother making weird knocking sounds inside as her weight shifted. The box loomed in the shadows so I draped my coat over it.

But Sue did not come home that night. When the small hours hit and I hadn't slept, I decided to close out the grades for my class. TeenMom hadn't submitted her final post—*Sum up your understanding of the importance of DNA-editing technology, hormone suppression, and Zeus-pod growth to the new reproductive possibilities of our age*—but I gave her an A anyway. She deserved it after all she had been through: the cling of a baby to her breast, the haze of those insomniac nights, the fight to get her thoughts out into the world. I wondered if she might enjoy my cake tin of pictures. Something to make her feel less alone, to offer a little guidance. I clicked on the address field.

She lived right outside the city, just where the hinterlands began, but still accessible by rail. From the train the high buildings of the city gave way to stretches of box stores and brick-and-mortar groceries. I disembarked in a wilderness of traffic lights and warehouses. As I walked, families came into focus around me, mothers and fathers and the children they were rearing, so different from the singles and groups of friends that roamed the city. Parents sat at picnic tables in small, concrete parks as their toddlers played with plastic toys in the dirt. They'd arranged food on the tables—sandwiches and juice boxes and bags of chips to share. They watched me pass and turned back to their business, neither friendly nor hostile, their attention held by the invisible lines of force that draw families together.

TeenMom's house was part of a line of well-appointed row houses, a gentrified area tucked between the industrial buildings on the adjoining blocks. The gate creaked as it closed behind me; a dog barked from down the road. A tiny bicycle stood chained to the fence, its handlebars shiny and new, awaiting its rider. I tightened my discount jacket at my neck. I'd thought it made me look professorial, its soft camel color studded with shiny brown buttons. But now I worried I looked kind of crazy, dressed up as something I was not and clutching my faded cake tin.

I mounted the steps and placed the tin on the doormat, its brown fibers emblazoned with the words "Home Sweet Home." Some instinct compelled me to lean over the rail and peer in the window. The interior was open plan, very modern; a living room led back to a kitchen bathed in track lights. And there she was, next to the island. She wore a turquoise robe and bunny slippers. She'd grown her hair out and she looked round and burnished, as though some particularly virulent strain of well-being had made her its vehicle. Before her sat a high chair, its back to me in a rectangle of white. She leaned down with a spoon. Someone appeared behind her, an older woman, thick and gentle-faced, and she too leaned down toward the high chair. She wiggled her fingers until the two women laughed at the baby's expression. I couldn't see what they were laughing at, but I smiled anyway, standing there looking in from the stoop.

AND THERE I WAS, months later, walking my baby home from the hospital. There was no father, of course: I'd had my procedure in the hinterlands, where bearing babies was considered an end in itself. There wasn't exactly a mother, either; it turned out something was wrong with my eggs, so all the contributions to my baby came from a bank. I must admit the whole enterprise caused me to see myself as a mutant creature, a cross between super technology and crass biology. I'd been created to escape the body's growth, the drag of personal history. But here I was, scratching at the pristine tablet of my life by choice, opening wounds that would never go away.

I'd shown up at the hospital near my apartment in full-blown labor, sending them scrambling to find anyone who'd delivered before. They stuck me with an ancient lady doctor whose crow face beamed from between my legs as I fought the agonies of contractions. I would've found the long labor unimaginable without all the natural childbirth books I'd ordered from antiquarian sites during my pregnancy. Still, the pain split the veil of perception to shreds, and as I wobbled along the sidewalk with my baby wrapped at my chest, the buildings around me blasted my eyes with their brightness. The people going by felt firm as peach stones, as though I'd never before sensed the presence of others, the world prior to giving birth a ghostlike echo of my new reality.

These passersby looked at me with pity, and what a sight I must have been, a smear of blood on my face and my baby pink with the raspy fluid of the womb against the bare skin of my throat. My legs rolled under me like numb stilts, shocked at what had passed between them. I let myself into the cold antechamber of my building and took the elevator to the fourth floor. Sue had moved out during my pregnancy, and no one would move in, given my circumstances. "You're certifiable," Sue had said, and she'd gone off to spend endless nights with Todd sipping vintage cocktails chilled by ice blocks he carved himself.

As I entered my apartment I sensed my mother in the living room, revived from her closet tomb during a weak moment in my third trimester. The baby had been kicking, and I wanted to put my mother's hand on my belly, to let her feel the hailstorm of tiny feet. Such an unimaginable thing, to have the space inside you give way to another life form, the bond between you unassailable. Now that she'd arrived, my mother and I could marvel together at the bones of her skull, separated into two small wings that had pressed together as she squeezed into the light.

My mother reclined before the single bright window in the living room. She sat unusually still, as though the passing of time couldn't touch her. I fell to my knees on the floor before her and slid my baby out of the wrap on my chest. "She's here," I said. "She's here." I cradled her spindly neck in my hand, her limbs splaying in surprise at the space opening around her as I placed her in my mother's lap.

"YES," my mother said, "A BABY! A BABY!"

My heart leaped, but then I noticed my mother was looking at me, not the baby at all, her eyes aglow with crystal zeal, my newborn child starting to slide off her legs. I smelled a strange smell, like wires burning, and my mother's hands opened and closed with a snap. I snatched the baby back; she sent up a lusty wail as my mother stared at me and bobbed her head, then bobbed it again, stuck in a loop of her programming.

Something drained out of me then, my sense of self driveling away, the emptiness left behind filled with the smell of the creature I clasped against me, the proteins of vernix and amniotic fluid baked into the warmth of her. I gazed down at her goblin face, still compressed from being inside me, her ears stuck to the sides of her head in diaphanous membranes. I could see it all before me: the way she'd grow as I would dwindle, the way we'd depend on one another with utter commitment until we wouldn't. I shivered as the feeling swept through me, a cold wind rushing through the cavernous space of my body.

I wished I had my cake tin. I had no idea what to do next. But I knew in all those clippings I would never see myself hunched over this ruddy, affronted baby with my mother slumped in her tacky, diamond-checked chair. I would have to start from scratch, a childhood made from nothing.

The baby quieted as she fell asleep on my chest, her cheek pressed in a sticky roll on my bare skin. I breathed the wax-spangled smell of her head, the broody atmosphere where her skin met the world. I wondered if Zeus had missed the weight of a baby in his arms. But daughters will dream what they will dream, and make their lives from it.

I gazed up at my mother, whose face had frozen in a wild grin. "Isn't she beautiful," I said.

And my mother nodded, and nodded again.

The Reformatory

Tananarive Due

Gracetown, Florida
Summer 1950

THE TRUCK RUMBLED to a stop at the far end of the campus, on the white side, within sight of the ghostly moonlit cornfields behind the fences. Chains clattered as the teenage boy beside Walter Stephens kicked his feet in rage. The older boy was the only one of the three of them whose legs and wrists were bound. The stocky Negro dorm master, Boone, had carried him out over his shoulder like he was a side of beef and dropped him into the bed of the white truck with a State of Florida seal. The boy hadn't stopped cussing the whole time they sped away from the dorm, the truck bumping over rocks and stumps and knots of grass, every building ahead a fright in the headlight beams. The older boy's lower lip was bleeding, or maybe his gums, the blood trickling on his chin. Neither Walter nor Redbone asked him what he'd done, but their small voices might have been lost inside the engine's rumble.

"Don't look at me, sissy," the teenager said, so Walter kept his eyes away.

The truck passed the kennels, where at least half a dozen dogs the size of red wolves barked from behind the wires. The dogs ran fast enough to keep pace as the truck drove past, eager for a chase. The dogs sounded angry, not playful. Walter wondered what the dogs did when they caught you.

When the truck lurched to a stop and the engine click-click-clicked before it went silent, Walter's heart bloated to his throat. The small wooden structure glowing in the bright headlights looked hardly bigger than a shed, painted bright white.

The Funhouse.

Two white boys sat on a bench outside the closed door while a white man in a billed cap kept watch over them. Walter thought maybe the Funhouse couldn't be so bad, with white boys here too—until a crack of leather striking flesh came from inside, and a boy's scream. Walter had never heard anyone scream that way except Mama, in her dying. His blood burned cold.

"Let's get 'im out," Boone said to Crutcher, the fussy, thin Negro man who was always at Boone's side. "Haddock wants him next."

Walter's body shook where he sat. Redbone scooted closer to him as Boone pulled down the truck bed's door with a sharp, rusty whine. They felt each other's hearts gallop with relief when Boone and Crutcher pulled the older boy out first and set him on his feet.

"I'm not goin' in there!" the boy yelled, lunging away. Boone popped him with a knee in the stomach so fast that Walter barely saw Boone move. The teenager doubled over while Boone and Crutcher pulled him to the Funhouse door. "You're all full of the devil!" the boy screamed.

Walter and Redbone looked at the white boys then, who in turn looked at them, their mirrors. Walter could swear he knew them although they had never met. The taller of the white boys, sandy-haired, also about twelve, was turning a small stone over in his palm. Walter wondered if he meant to use it as a weapon, but it was too small to be anything except a charm. Would he carry it through his whipping? Walter wished he had a stone to hold too.

The Funhouse door opened just as Crutcher signaled Walter and Redbone out of the truck. They climbed out like their limbs were stone. Walter saw only glimpses of a bare light bulb inside, the warden's silhouette, another man behind him. Boone dragged in the wailing teenager while a white man led a young white boy out.

"Negroes wait on the other side," Crutcher said, gesturing.

While he walked, Walter turned his head to lock eyes with the white boys as long as he could, as if they could stare a plan into each other's minds. But soon he and Redbone were on the dark side of the shed, where six empty metal chairs waited, askew. Crutcher straightened the chairs to a line and gestured for them to sit. Then he went off to pace by the fence, lighting a cigar. Behind him, corn stalks shook in the breeze. Walter's knees still trembled after he sat. Warden Haddock was lecturing inside the shed, but his voice was too low to make out. Walter heard only the sobbing.

"Maybe they'll get tired," Redbone said.

"They?" Walter's body tensed so much that his chair's legs rattled.

"Two or three hold you, one beats you. They lay you on a table. Take turns sometimes."

"No talking. Talking's what got you here," Crutcher said, hushed. "If you can't learn here, where will you learn?"

"I've learned, sir," Walter said.

"Me too, sir."

"Shush—you haven't. Best you learn now. It's a shame for the new one, but I hope you see now to stay far away from the Funhouse."

Walter had planned to avoid the Funhouse as soon as he heard about the Reformatory's whipping shed, and now he was here on his first night.

"Yes, sir, I see," Walter said. His throat was crammed with tears. He wanted to say he was sorry for what he'd done, but he couldn't remember: was this punishment for asking Redbone if anyone ever tried to run away, or because he'd eaten the apple tart while they were working in the kitchen? Was it because he'd been late to the dormitory, or because he'd kicked Lyle McCormack on Tobacco Road? He couldn't count everything he was sorry for. He was sorrier he had to spend six months at the Reformatory when he couldn't imagine six days, or six minutes. He was sorriest that Papa had been run out of town and Mama had died. His whole life was sorry. He'd barely kicked Lyle McCormack, and Lyle himself said he was fine. If only Lyle's father hadn't seen. If only Lyle hadn't looked at Walter's sister, Gloria, that way and touched her arm like he had a right to.

"Don't go in there arguin'. Learn the lesson, say you're sorry," Crutcher said. "Can't be like your daddy, fighting battles you can't win. His way don't work here."

Walter looked at Crutcher, startled. He couldn't make out his face, so far off at the fence.

"You know my papa?" Walter said. "Sir?" He didn't answer, so Walter asked again. "Mr. Crutcher, you know my—"

"'Course I do—from the mill," Crutcher said. "Nobody in three counties don't know the name Walt Stephens." Walter heard admiration in his voice. Crutcher's orange cigar ash flared to the ground. "You two choose which one goes first. One of you's next."

Perspiration sprang up on Walter everywhere at once.

"I'll go first," Redbone said, resigned. "Waiting's harder."

Inside the shed, the floor creaked. A sharp whistle, then a lash. The teenager yelped, crying. His whipping had begun. Two lashes.

Due

Three. Four. Five. The higher the number, each as hard or worse as the previous, the more Walter could feel his own shoulders, his knees, wincing with each one. The sound rocked through him. He thought the twentieth lash would end it, but it didn't. Or the thirtieth. But after thirty-five lashes, when tears dripped from Walter's face, the whipping stopped. The sobbing was gone too, and silence was worse. Walter sucked at the air. The chair's seat beneath him was so damp, he couldn't tell if he'd wet himself the way he had when he first stood in the warden's office that morning. His terror of discovery then felt silly and long ago.

After Crutcher went to help bring the teenage boy out, Walter stared at the cornfield, wondering if there was a place to scale the fence, or a hole someone might have left unrepaired in overgrown brush. He would have cut off his arm to know. He would have tried to outrun dogs.

"They give you a wood chip to bite on," Redbone said. "Don't spit it out. Better use it."

Crutcher signaled, and Redbone rose. Walter burned to say something to him, but he couldn't make his mouth move and Redbone didn't look at him anyway. Boone and a white man dragged the teenager out of the Funhouse by the shoulders.

Walter's chair rattled when he craned to see the older boy being lifted back into the truck. He was relieved when the boy bucked and cried out again. Boone clapped the truck's panel shut and patted the door, and the white man drove the boy away, toward parts of the campus Walter did not know. Then Boone pulled Redbone's arm, and Redbone vanished behind the clapboard wall. Behind the closed door.

Crutcher strolled back toward Walter, but farther away this time, a good fifteen yards, so he could watch the white boys on one side and Walter on the other. Walter knew he could easily outrun Crutcher at this distance, if only he knew where to go.

Inside, the warden's voice sounded jovial, as if he were meeting an old friend.

No delays. No scuffles. Redbone's lashes began right away.

Fire. That was the feeling of the strap. Walter felt it in Redbone's scream, loud and anguished and somehow surprised. By the second lash, the surprise in his scream was gone. For his third lash, Redbone must have gritted down hard on his wood chip, so his scream sounded more muffled. But whether they were loud or soft, Redbone's screams scraped Walter's ears raw and wrung out tears that drowned his face. His chair legs clattered when he sobbed. If Crutcher heard him, he didn't let on.

"Mama?" Walter whispered to the shadowed corn. "I need you. I can't do this. I can't."

The breeze picked up and dry corn stalks whispered, and Walter remembered when such things used to feel like a sign from Mama. If he saw a red bird (Mama's favorite). If he heard a creak on the floorboards when his eyes were closed. But whispering corn wasn't enough now.

"Please, Mama. I know maybe it's hard to come, but I need you."

Spirits roamed free in this place, which might mean other spirits could come and go. He felt the spirits all around him. He'd smelled the smoke as Boone drove him past where the shed had burned down in 1920. In the kitchen, he'd felt flicks of knifepoint to show him how many boys had died from a kitchen blade. Before Walter closed his eyes and wished him away, he'd seen a boy charred from head to foot standing over his bed. Then Boone had come to wake Walter and Redbone to take them to the Funhouse—far scarier than any spirit.

"Mama—please."

A *ping* sounded just below Walter's pinkie where he was resting his weight on his chair. He heard it both from the metal and between his ears, amplified, a pulse. To be sure, he waited to feel it again. *Ping.*

So many feelings came at once: chiefly anger. *Why hadn't she come to him this way before now?* But anger was quickly followed by tearful relief, and a joy like none he'd ever known, like breathing a new kind of oxygen. Then all of that gave way to pain again.

"Why I gotta' be here, Mama? I can't do this. It ain't fair." It was as if she were sitting in the empty seat beside him, almost as if she had never been gone.

Another *ping*, and this time Walter cupped his hand over the vibration so it tickled his palm. In that touch, Walter felt how sorry Mama was to see him like this, how she wanted to help, but couldn't. *Ping.* This time, he felt her arms wrap around him and sway with him.

This isn't everything, he heard Mama's voice say inside his ear. *There's more ahead for you than this. This is only a moment.*

Redbone must have dropped his wood chip. He howled.

"This isn't everything. There's more than this," Walter said.

The *ping* tickled Walter's palm, and his ears fogged, the howling far away.

TRUE TO ITS CARNIVAL NICKNAME, the Funhouse looked twice as big on the inside, an endlessly long shed, at its center the table, lit from an overhead bulb as if it were a main stage. A transistor radio on the shelf by the door played a cheerful song like a county fair; a fiddle and a guitar and a singer who sounded like a cowboy. Laughter snapped Walter's head around. Two shirtless, sweating white men were dealing cards over a stack of crates in the corner, their bare bellies jiggling. Everyone else was busy: Crutcher wiping down the table beneath the light, Boone locking the door behind him, and Warden Haddock rinsing his leather strap in a small sink. Walter tried not to notice how the water washed down pink. Methodically, Warden Haddock wiped the thick strap with a towel.

This isn't everything. There is more than this.

"Not off to a good start, are you?" Warden Haddock said as he wiped. His face, already narrow, hollowed at the cheeks.

"No, sir." Walter could barely speak through the coat of phlegm in his throat.

"You know what you did wrong?"

Walter longed to argue, but he remembered Crutcher's warning. "Asking stupid questions, sir. I'm sorry, sir."

Warden Haddock laid his strap down on the table and picked up a lighted cigarette from a clay ashtray. Walter held a wild hope he might say, *Well, never mind all this, then—go'n back to bed.* Instead, Warden Haddock studied Walter with his eyebrows raised, as if he might have heard wrong.

"'Stupid questions'?" Warden Haddock said. Exaggerated, the phrase seemed monstrous. "That what you call it?"

Boone made a chuffing sound, glaring at him. Another mistake in a day of mistakes. Walter dared not answer.

"A 'stupid' question would be 'Does the sun rise in the west?'" Warden Haddock said. "'Do pigs like slop?' Those are stupid questions. Way I hear it, 'less you're callin' Boone a liar, you were asking questions about how to run away."

In the corner of his eye, Walter noticed the men at the crates flexing their arms, exercising their fingers. They had put their cards down. They were preparing to hurt him.

"Not for *me* to run, sir," Walter said. "I was just asking if anybody ever did. . . ." Walter's voice dropped away. Crutcher had told him not to argue. Keep his mouth shut.

"Why would you want to know if a thing is possible, Walter Stephens, 'less you thought you might want to try it? Explain that to me."

Due

Everyone's eyes came to Walter. Under the room's gaze, his mind spilled empty.

Warden Haddock picked up the leather strap again, wrapping it from elbow to palm.

"Like . . ." Walter imagined the *ping* from Mama beneath his hand, as if she were whispering in his ear: ". . . like how in picture shows, people fly to outer space and can look down on the whole Earth. Or how Joe Friday chases down crooks on *Dragnet*. I ain't never gonna be on no rocket ship, no police detective, but I still want to hear it like a story."

The room was still while the men waited to hear what Warden Haddock would say.

After a time, the warden nodded. "'Like a story.' A kind of fairy tale."

"Yessir," Walter said.

"You believe that, Boone?"

Please please please please please.

Boone shrugged. "Dunno, boss. That's what they both said. Like it was just a story."

"Bullshit," one of the white men said under his breath.

"Stories are dangerous, Stephens," Warden Haddock said. "They can get you hurt bad. Get you killed. Your friend the storyteller just got thirty lashes. It's not his first time here, and he should know better. I have to teach you too, and I'm not sure yet how many licks that'll take. But however the Lord leads me, from now on, if you're smart—and I think maybe you are—you're not gonna want to hear no more stories."

"No, sir." Walter's words were only air whistling between his chattering teeth.

Crutcher gently cupped Walter's elbow like an usher leading him to the front of the church, and Walter's body seized up, but he walked with Crutcher anyway—one step, two, three—toward the table where he would be whipped. Crutcher was gentle enough to fool him into wondering if he might be spared. Hadn't Mama's messages to him already been a miracle?

"Gimme your shirt." Walter hesitated just long enough for Crutcher to say, "You don't want to wear it. Fabric gets in the skin." For the first time, Walter thought of his skin breaking; not bruises, not welts, but slashed-open flesh. Walter looked at Crutcher with pleading eyes: *You know my papa and you know this ain't right*, and Crutcher's eyes blinked away.

Boone tugged at Walter's shirt impatiently, so Walter quickly pulled on the buttons, trying to tame his fingers' strange dancing. Walter heard shuffling, all of the men moving to their places, penning him in. Ready to catch him if he ran. Warden Haddock's boots snapped closer against the floorboards, thunder in Walter's ears.

"He always so polite and quiet?" Warden Haddock said.

"Seems like he was raised nice enough." Was Crutcher arguing for him?

"I don't think you wanna bring up his rearin'," Warden Haddock said, and Crutcher's face puckered as he tried to hold his expression blank. Crutcher wasn't the only one in Gracetown who knew Papa's name. "But I'll say this: he's lucky I'm the warden and not some of those country boys, or he'd be out in a swamp with the Klan instead of here. My boys are already grumbling. So don't try to say I don't play fair."

"I don't know a man fairer, boss," Boone said. "White or colored. That's the truth."

"I'll take it one more step," Warden Haddock said, and spat to build up anticipation like Reverend Jenkins turned to his spittoon when he was encouraged by the excitement from his flock. "I'd bet five dollars that gal was never raped by nobody, white or Negro."

The walls seemed to vibrate. The two white men groaned angrily, and Boone and Crutcher shifted, uncomfortable, the amen corner silent now. The room felt weighted down.

Due

"Know what? Make that ten dollars." Warden Haddock said. "What you think, Walter Stephens? Did your daddy rape that white lady?"

Walter's mouth was so dry that his tongue and cheeks felt glued to his lips. He could not open his mouth. To speak, he thought, might mean dying. White men talking about rape always led to a rope. That's what Papa had said right before he climbed in the trunk of the pastor's car.

"Sir, the boy don't know nothin' 'bout that," Crutcher said, quiet as an undertaker.

"He's not shy." Warden Haddock nudged Walter with the tip of his boot, heavy pressure on his bare toes. Walter felt one of his toe joints crack. "Go on and say. Did your daddy rape that white lady?"

The word *rape* was profane. The first time he'd heard it had been last year, when the sheriff came looking for Papa. He'd asked the older boys at school what rape was even though Gloria wouldn't tell him. *It's when a girl doesn't want to, but you force her anyway*, the sage eighth-grader, Pastor Jenkins's son, had said. *Sinners and cowards and drunks do that.*

"No, sir," Walter whispered. "My daddy wouldn't hurt nobody. He'd never do that. He ain't a sinner or coward or drunk."

By the way the warden's head canted to one side as if to see him in better lighting, Walter realized he should have thought before he spoke. Only fright had made his words tumble out. Neither Crutcher nor Boone would look at Walter. Crutcher took one step away, pretending to search his vest pocket, as if hearing talk of the white lady would conjure her.

"So, you think she lied?"

"I think like you think, Warden Haddock." Walter knew better than to say *lie*.

Warden Haddock slapped Walter on the back hard enough to sting and then rubbed the spot to soothe it. "There you go," he said. "Everybody knows it. Just a bunch of vile stories the growers put Lucy up to cuz of all his union talk. Probably paid her and her loudmouth daddy and mama a pretty penny. All of y'all know it and won't say. And leastways, I won't visit the sins of the father on the son. The son pays for his own sins. Ain't that right, Walter Stephens?" Warden Haddock continued to rub at the spot on his shoulder until a new alarm grew in Walter. Slowly, Warden Haddock slid his hand away.

"I don't know for sho what my daddy did or didn't do, sir," Walter said, and his heart died a thousand deaths, and he wondered if somewhere in his exile in Chicago, Papa might have heard him.

"Hush. Yes you do," Warden Haddock said. "A young man stands by his convictions. Hop on up on the table. The good Lord has seen fit to give me this opportunity to steer you to the right path."

An angry white man yanked Walter so hard that the tabletop dug into his stomach and made him lose his breath. The man's red caterpillar eyebrows frowned. Walter smelled sour beer on the man's breath, in his sweat; he worked drunk most nights—

—like the men who had started the fire in 1920.

All thirteen boys had burned to death, screaming to drunken ears. Knowing what he shouldn't made Walter dizzy.

The memory of Mama's most recent touch gave Walter the strength to pull his leg high enough to try to hoist himself onto the wooden table. It was truly as if he'd never worked his body before, every part difficult to manage, like his newborn cousin Jackie, who had been named for Jackie Robinson. He thought of Jackie's wobbly arms and legs as he nearly slipped from the plank, which was slick with sweat.

No, not sweat. The sharp, prickly scent was blood.

He looked behind him to the mud-splattered wall, and realized the tiny dark dots in random patterns were not mud. Blood patterns were sprayed like paint droplets against the dull planks. He would bleed here. His blood might fly.

Due

"Take this," Crutcher said, and shoved a thick, uneven wood chip into Walter's hand. The chip was dry, fresh from a storage bin. Walter's fingers shook around it. Crutcher leaned closer and whispered in smoky breath, "Bite down. Lie still as you can. It'll be over quicker."

Walter didn't know when he had started crying. Warden Haddock made a *tsk tsk tsk* sound and Walter bit back a sob. Now that his shirt was off, the room seemed as cold as the freezer in the kitchen.

"What you waitin' for, Walter Stephens?" Warden Haddock said. "Lie down."

"Do what he say, nigger," Boone said.

When Walter felt Boone grab his left arm, he hurriedly shoved his wood chip into his mouth. The wood almost jostled loose as three men grabbed and arranged his body with rough hands, but Walter raised his head high so the chip would fall against his molars. He imagined ants or wood mites crawling in his mouth, but his teeth sank into the soft wood, fused. Walter's hot breath hissed in and out against the wood, but his jaw held on so hard it ached. His whole body heaved with his breathing.

The edge of the table pressed against Walter's collarbone—only his neck muscles kept his head from dangling forward—and Walter suddenly knew that boys had died on this table during their beatings, their voice boxes crushed and necks snapped during careless handling. No, he would not move. He would do as Crutcher had said and lie still. He would do as Redbone had said and bite on the wood chip. He would remember what Mama told him.

"There is more than this," Walter whispered against the wood in his mouth.

The floor creaked under the warden's boot. A low whistle and snap sounded above Walter, and then pain tore across his back, as surely as if it had claws. Most of his scream stayed bottled in his throat. His jaw clamped down so hard on the wood chip that he was sure he'd loosened all his teeth. Just as Walter began to think the pain wasn't so bad, the numbness wore off his back in a wave and he felt that his skin must have surely peeled in two.

Walter writhed and screamed. Then came the next blow, laid across the first. He would have spat out the wood if he could, if it weren't so fixed to his teeth, because pain was choking him. Wild in him.

"Stop—" Walter tried to say, muffled, but the whistle and snap sounded, and his body went rigid, and when the lash came it seemed to snap his spine apart. Walter's head flung right and left as he screamed, and if not for the wood chip he might have bitten his tongue off when his chin hit the edge of the table so hard he saw sparks before his eyes.

By the fourth lash, or the fifth—he lost count, one fire burning into the next—his throat was raw and his jaw pulsed and he was sure his back must be a solid pool of blood streaming to the floor. Pastor Jenkins's hellfire could be no worse than this! Boys got beat like this for being late to curfew or fighting or talking too much at night? Boys got beat like this for everyday things his teacher might rap his wrist with a ruler for? The wrongness rang in his head.

"This ain't right," Walter tried to say—a mush against the saliva-drenched chip in his mouth, which still would not budge no matter how much he tried to scream. "This ain't right!"

His outburst met another lash—a worse one. His skin melted open beneath the cutting leather, and he knew it was far worse than the rest as he flopped on the table. To hold him in place, a man clamped each arm harder on either side of him, another held both of his legs. The edge of the table dug into his throat, and for the first time Walter stopped screaming. His nose was clogged. The new panic from not breathing was worse than the pain, so he remembered to slow his hitching breaths. Don't move. Don't move. Don't move. Soon, the men loosened their grip a bit and he could shift his neck enough to keep the table from crushing his throat.

For the next five lashes, maybe six, he whimpered but could not scream. He was melting from the table, beneath Boone's muddy work boots and Warden Haddock's pointed shiny snakeskin ones, beneath the floor, into the red-brown soil, past the long-forgotten ashes from the fire in 1920, all the way to the bones buried at the Reformatory cemetery everyone called Boot Hill. Vibrating pain coiled across his back, but no pain could touch him where he was buried in the soil. His body was far above him, the world black.

Kindred spirits awaited him here: boys who had been afraid of beatings and dogs, whose skin had been torn or charred, their flesh stabbed, whose bones had snapped, spirits circling the site of their shared desecration. They rose with a stink of the wrong done to them, and he could almost see them in the dark, straining to have their faces remembered.

I see you, he told them, and it almost wasn't a lie because sometimes he did see what might be shadows of noses and chins in rows around him. *I see you*. And when he did not see their faces, he saw their stories: Jim, who had run away once too many times and his family never saw him again after they found a note from the sheriff tacked to their front door. Jesse, whose family had sold him to the Reformatory for fifty dollars because they thought it would teach him not to sass back. Russell, who went truant each fall to help his uncle paint houses. And Reynaldo and Justin and Emory and John, who had done nothing beyond being left behind by their parents, torn away by drink or sickness or death, just like him. The dead boys were called every name except Murdered: accident or oversight or cautionary tale.

"He fainted dead away," said a voice he remembered was Crutcher's.

Walter heard, but did not feel, the final lash do its unholy work across his tattered skin.

"I've got a headache anyways," the warden said.

A fiddle's whine from the radio niggled at Walter's ear, bringing light through his closed eyelids. Even half senseless and full of rage and pain, he knew better than to open his eyes, or the warden might change his mind and keep whipping him. And if the warden spoke a single word to him, Walter worried he would spit in his face. Oh yes, he would.

There is more than this. In the grainy light of his returning, Walter Stephens heard his heartbeat, and the frantic pumping helped him remember: no, he wasn't like the sullen ghosts who roamed this place. The warden hadn't killed him—not yet—and Walter vowed he never would, just like Papa had outfoxed the lynch mob.

He was alive.

There is more than this.

He would learn.

There is more than this.

Like Papa, he would find a way to be free.

Due

What Used to Be Caracas

Mike McClelland

Basseterre, St. Kitts and Nevis
17.3026° N, 62.7177° W

HUMBOLDT NOTES:

Time is the most important thing in human life, for what is pleasure after
the departure of time? And the most consolatory, since pain, when pain
has passed, is nothing. Time is the wheel-rut in which we roll on toward
eternity, conducting us to the incomprehensible. In its progress there is a
ripening power, and it ripens us the more, and the more powerfully, when
we duly estimate it. Listen to its voice, do not waste it, but regard it as the
highest finite good, in which all finite things are resolved.

—*A. Humboldt*

EXPEDITION NOTES:

The field technician must note that the goal of this expedition is to expand
upon the work of his great-great-great-great-great-great-uncle, Alexander
von Humboldt (a surname the family later changed at Ellis Island to

Humbletrot). Humboldt used ecology, geography, and anthropology to survey this portion of Venezuela in 1799. The field team—which consists of the field technician, a volcanologist, a teuthologist, a hydrologist, an ethnoarcheologist, and an aviator—has hypothesized that Humboldt discovered information that predicted the Erasure, which would occur nearly a quarter millennium later, but destroyed most of his personal journals to spare his descendants the psychological trauma that such knowledge would impart.

In expanding upon the work of Humboldt, this expedition aims to give back to humanity what Humboldt regarded as its most precious resource: time. One of catastrophe's more insidious consequences is that it denies human beings the freedom to think, to explore, to enjoy, and to expand. Survival is an activity that demands constant engagement. The Erasure robbed humankind of time and, as a result, of any power it possessed.

The field technician must also note that this report is presented according to the rules set forth in the Post-Erasure Manual of Style (PEMS), and as such, out of respect for the billions of lives lost during the Erasure, the field technician will not refer to himself in the first person outside of the PEMS-prescribed attribution of authorship and will address his colleagues by the common terms of their genders and/or occupations.

—*E. Humbletrot*

Simón Bolívar International Airport, Venezuela
10.6021° N, 66.9955° W

HUMBOLDT NOTES:
This view of a living nature where man is nothing is both odd and sad. Here, in a fertile land, in an eternal greenness, you search in vain for

traces of man; you feel you are carried into a different world from the one you were born into.

—*A. Humboldt*

FIELD NOTES:

The airport ruins sit between the former coastline and the northern edge of what used to be Caracas. The once-verdant landscape is cracked and white, though the field technician must note he may be using the word "cracked" because it is phonetically similar to "Caracas." Indeed, there are few actual cracks in the terrain. Rather it is ridged and occasionally pocked. Not cracked.

The only remaining flora is based around the harenam at Catia La Mar, due east of the airport. Though Venezuela's attempt to import fresh water proved disastrous, resulting in dry, bright blue salt pits such as this one at Catia La Mar, it is that attempt that has allowed life to remain here in the form of these two species of pale green, lichen-like flora (previously undocumented species recorded here as *Caldas* and *Lussac*).

Sadly, there is no evidence of any living fauna, despite speculation that several species remained in the area around the Venezuelan Coastal Range directly west of the airport. The peaks of the range have taken on the hunched, grey appearance typical of mountains affected by the salt storms that hit coastal areas in the weeks directly following the Erasure.

—*E. Humbletrot*

Henri Pittier National Park
10.3819° N, 67.6185° W

HUMBOLDT NOTES:

Mere communion with nature, mere contact with the free air, exercises a soothing yet comforting and strengthening influence on the wearied mind, calms the storm of passion, and softens the heart when shaken by sorrow to its inmost depths.

—A. Humboldt

FIELD NOTES:

Henri Pittier National Park is the site of the first known cavecanem, which still burns bright. It has been established that the Pittier Cavecanem's early arrival was due to the nine rivers flowing within the park's borders. The rivers crisscrossed over the volatile tectonic area where the Caribbean Plate meets the South American Plate. As a result, when all of those rivers became salt, they ignited, causing the unending burn typical of a cavecanem. The Pittier Cavecanem borders the Valencia Harenam, making for vibrant vistas of orange and blue if one can find high ground and endure the deadly temperatures.

The field team spent several days analyzing the Pittier Cavecanem and, as predicted, found it empty.

The park's flora and fauna are all long dead, most tragically (in the biased opinion of the field technician) the 500 species of birds that made their homes in Henri Pittier National Park. This number included 22 endemic species.

The field technician must note that, as a birdwatcher and amateur ornithologist, his account of Henri Pittier National Park may be compromised by emotional distress.

Still, nature has managed to counter that distress with the slimmest silver line of hope. Three green-blue eggs were discovered in the stump of a tree along what used to be the El Limón River.

—E. Humbletrot

McClelland

San Francisco de Yare
10.1794° N, 66.7248° W

HUMBOLDT NOTES:

The philosophical study of nature endeavors, in the vicissitudes of phenomena, to connect the present with the past.

—*A. Humboldt*

FIELD NOTES:

San Francisco de Yare is where it becomes challenging to differentiate
between the science of the Erasure and the myth surrounding it. But,
given the goals of this expedition, that challenge is a welcome one.

This particular myth concerns the Dancing Devils of Yare. There
was a saying in the area: "If there is no money nor believers to carry the
Blessed Sacrament in Procession, then come devils." Each year, on the
day of Corpus Christi, the citizens of San Francisco de Yare dressed
up as devils and processed through the streets, carrying the Blessed
Sacrament and collecting money as they danced along.

This happened every year from 1749 right up until the year before
the Erasure, when bad weather, disorganized believers, and a financial
crisis led to the cancellation of the procession. According to reports from
the now-deceased local population, this resulted in the coming of the
devils. Specifically, Lucifer and Abaddon, who are said to have risen
from Hell through San Francisco de Yare's twin cavecanems.

The field team spent nearly two weeks analyzing the Lucifer Cavecanem and the Abaddon Cavecanem and, as predicted, found them
empty. However, though there was no proof of demonic activity, the
team did find evidence that something had in fact emerged from the
cavecanems here.

—*E. Humbletrot*

Cagua
10.1757° N, 67.4576° W

HUMBOLDT NOTES:
Nature offers unceasingly the most novel and fascinating objects for learning.

—*A. Humboldt*

FIELD NOTES:
Cagua's history is one of moderate success. Before everyone died, of course.

Founded by Spaniards in 1620 (though indigenous people lived here long before, so "founded" is a stretch, but that was the way of the pre-Erasure world), Cagua sustained itself for 500 years.

Cagua gets its name from the native Cumanagoto word for "snail." Interestingly, this name is more appropriate for the city's post-Erasure state, as it is now notable for the rivers of snail shells that flood what used to be Cagua's streets.

According to the field team's research, snails flooded into Cagua because it was in the rare position of sitting in a valley surrounded by bodies of water to the north, south, east, and west. These were, of course, the Caribbean Sea to the north, Lago de Valencia to the west, Embalse de Zuata to the east, and Laguna Taguaiguai to the south.

Research suggests that the "Snail Rivers of Cagua" could potentially serve as a tourist attraction or as a destination for pilgrimage, as the unique hue of the shells of the millions of dead moon snails causes the entire city to glow brilliant pink-gold in the daylight and silver-blue in the moonlight.

However, this potential relies on several significant factors, beyond the obvious need to first stabilize the post-Erasure economy.

These include the cooling of the Cagua Cavecanem, the building of a sustainable fresh water recycling system, and the removal of some of Cagua's ghastly industrial architecture, which detracts greatly from the majesty of the Snail Rivers.

The field team spent several days analyzing the Cagua Cavecanem and, as predicted, found it empty.

—*E. Humbletrot*

Los Teques
10.3492° N, 67.0345° W

HUMBOLDT NOTES:

In considering the study of physical phenomena, not merely in its bearings on the material wants of life, but in its general influence on the intellectual advancement of mankind, we find its noblest and most important result to be a knowledge of the chain of connection, by which all natural forces are linked together, and made mutually dependent upon each other; and it is the perception of these relations that exalts our views and ennobles our enjoyments.

—*A. Humboldt*

FIELD NOTES:

The field technician must note that a miracle has occurred! One of the three eggs discovered in Henri Pittier National Park hatched this morning in the sock compartment of the field technician's suitcase. The hatchling resembles a baby chicken, though it is dark grey. Given the color of the egg and the characteristics of the baby bird, the field technician can comfortably hypothesize that he is now in the possession of a living grey tinamou, a species thought to be extinct following the

Erasure. Though the general aim of this expedition is observation rather than collection, the field technician will make an exception and bring the creature back to Basseterre.

The birth occurred in Los Teques, which is most notable for its proximity to the Miranda Cavecanem. The Miranda Cavecanem is a rare high-altitude cavecanem and is thought to have been formed when a shard of the South American Plate splintered in the forming of the Pittier Cavecanem and allowed magma to shoot up into the post-Erasure salt beds of the former Rio San Pedro. The field team spent one week analyzing the Miranda Cavecanem and, as predicted, found it empty.

Los Teques has no surviving flora or fauna. However, the illusion of life remains as the metro still runs on schedule between Caracas and Los Teques. The system was automated shortly before the Erasure, and the red and grey trains still arrive and leave on time even though they are, of course, empty.

—*E. Humbletrot*

San Juan de los Morros
9.9127° N, 67.3615° W

HUMBOLDT NOTES:
I saw with regret (and all scientific men have shared this feeling) that while the number of accurate instruments was daily increasing, we were still ignorant.

—*A. Humboldt*

FIELD NOTES:
From the sky, San Juan de los Morros has little in common with this expedition's other destinations. While there are some striking light blue

harenams in the area, caused when local manmade reservoirs turned into salt and combusted against scorching pockets of underground gas, there were no other large bodies of water nearby before the Erasure, so there are none of the salt pits or massive, sizzling cavecanems that mark the other locations. Instead, a twenty-meter-tall statue of San Juan Bautista surrounded by a misty orange haze is what visibly remains of San Juan de los Morros.

There used to be hot springs here, and it is thought that when the Erasure turned their water to salt, the salt reacted with the magma that had previously heated the water in the springs and formed dozens of glowing holes in the ground. These are collectively called the Micro-cavecanems of San Juan Bautista. However, our team has been unable to confirm the exact origins of the microcavecanems, as they are not as hot or as uniform in shape as their brethren (which has allowed some of the salt within them to cool enough to blow in the wind, causing the salty haze that hovers around the statue's feet).

The field team spent several days analyzing the Microcavecanems of San Juan Bautista and, as predicted, found them empty.

The grey tinamou continues to grow, surviving on a small amount of the field technician's puréed leftovers. The field technician must note that the bird prefers to sleep in its sock compartment during the day and awaken in the evening, which is in direct opposition to the behavior of the diurnal, pre-Erasure tinamou. As such, it has been christened Night-bird. Stranger still, Nightbird has yet to consume any water, apparently sustaining itself off of the small amount found in what it's been fed.

While in San Juan de los Morros, the field team dined on arepas, which originated in the area, in honor of the city's former inhabitants.

—*E. Humbletrot*

Higuerote
10.4685° N, 66.1059° W

HUMBOLDT NOTES:
What we glean from travelers' vivid descriptions has a special charm; whatever is far off and suggestive excites our imagination; such pleasures tempt us far more than anything we may daily experience in the narrow circle of sedentary life.

—A. Humboldt

FIELD NOTES:
The bright blue salt of the Harenam de los Piratas makes it appear as if Higuerote is still perched on a beach. Of course, it is not, as there are no beaches left. Viewed from above, one can see the blue salt quickly fade to the dirty off-white variety so typical of what used to be the ocean.

Higuerote held a special place in the heart of Alexander von Humboldt, as it was mentioned in the Spanish explorer Alonso de Ojeda's notes from his 1499 voyage. Humboldt, who, like Ojeda, was exploring on behalf of the Spanish royal family, visited Higuerote almost 300 years to the day after his predecessor. Even with the recent addition of the bright blue harenam, Higuerote is geographically rather bland and it is surprising that both Ojeda and Humboldt would mention it in their notes.

The field technician must note that Humboldt's idolization of Ojeda is a blemish on his ancestor's otherwise sterling history, as Ojeda was a rather unsavory individual, having enslaved and sold a great number of the indigenous people he came in contact with on his journey.

Nightbird has grown to the size of a small chicken and has become the unofficial mascot of the field team. The teuthologist, who studied general zoology extensively before turning his focus solely to cephalopods, informed the team that Nightbird is a male. He's a chirpy but otherwise sedentary creature (Nightbird, not the teuthologist, who is rather taciturn), content to nest in the field technician's socks and occasionally squawk for refreshments. The hydrologist, being the only member of the field team with a surviving spouse, joked that Nightbird reminds her of her wife, giving the team a rare shared chuckle.

The field team spent over a week analyzing the Bahia Cavecanem and the Tacarigua Cavecanem and, as predicted, found them empty.

—*E. Humbletrot*

Altagracia de Orituco
9.8563° N, 66.3736° W

HUMBOLDT NOTES:
The most dangerous worldview is the worldview of those who have not viewed the world.

—*A. Humboldt*

FIELD NOTES:
Microcavecanems, those tiny trenches of glowing, superheated salt, are the defining feature of Altagracia de Orituco. The volcanologist and hydrologist believe that the microcavecanems here were formed when the miniscule amounts of moisture that remained in the tiny fossilized skeletons that formed the limestone formations of the Morros de Macaira Natural Monument turned to salt, causing the remaining parts to crumble and fall into the earth in small sections, where they hit either magma or gas and formed these small, swimming pool–sized cavecanems.

The field team spent three weeks analyzing the Orituco Microcavecanems and, as predicted, found them all empty.

The Guanapito Harenam, formed by a former reservoir just north of the city, provided a relatively cool area for the team to make camp amongst the heat of the hundreds of sizzling microcavecanems. The ethnoarcheologist took Nightbird with her (leashed, of course) as she went to investigate the city's remains, and shockingly reported that Nightbird enthusiastically munched the blue salt of the Guanapito Harenam as they strolled. The ethnoarcheologist brought a sample back to camp where the hydrologist studied it, discovering that in addition to sodium and chlorine, the salt contained a high level of hydrogen. Though it seems unlikely given the extremely short amount of time for evolution to have taken place, the field team has tentatively hypothesized that Nightbird is able to survive on minuscule amounts of water, instead gathering nutrients from the very salt that killed his brethren.

This information about Nightbird is enough to change what is known about post-Erasure evolution. However, every member of the team acknowledges the necessity for discretion. Humanity has suffered so many shocks in a short period of time, and the pessimism, fear, and cynicism that resulted from the Erasure necessitate keeping our feathery companion a secret for now.

—E. Humbletrot

Los Roques Archipelago
11.8575° N, 66.7575° W

HUMBOLDT NOTES:
With most animals, as with man, the alertness of the senses diminishes after years of work, after domestic habits and progress of culture.

—A. Humboldt

FIELD NOTES:

The field team arrived at the Gran Roque Cavecanem and, as predicted, found it to be inhabited by a massive, tentacled hell creature.

It is at this point, reader, that the field technician must admit that he has not been entirely forthcoming. His hope is that by this point in the report you have become so charmed by his polite catchphrase ("the field technician must note") and his salt-chomping tinamou mascot that you are now willing to believe—or at least lend your ear to—the most bizarre of circumstances. Still, the field technician must note that he has not lied. Omission was his sole deception.

The members of this expedition are well aware that it is the opinion of the leadership in the surviving cities of Basseterre, Malé, Kuwait City, Valletta, and Doha that God and not science caused the Erasure, as alluded to in Psalms 107:34 and Jeremiah 17:6. Our official objective in exploring post-Erasure Venezuela was to ascertain the suitability of the area for repopulation, pilgrimage, or at least tourism, like similar expeditions around what used to be Reykjavík and what used to be Jakarta. The field technician has previously withheld the following information because he and his team believe that God and science are not unknown to one another. The field technician hopes that the reader has gained confidence in him by this point in the report and will absorb the following information with the open mind it requires.

Before this expedition even began, the team hypothesized that this, the former Los Roques Archipelago, referred to in pre-Erasure days as "the new Bermuda Triangle," would be the location of the creature that in all likelihood caused the Erasure. This hypothesis was based on the assorted notes of Alexander von Humboldt, the abundance of the otherwise-rare cavecanems in the area, and on mythological informa-tion gathered by the ethnoarcheologist and her team back in Basseterre. Privately, the team has been referring to the creature as the Eraser, though it has also been referred to as Cthulhu, Kraken, Leviathan, and Ragnarök. These nicknames must be taken with a grain of salt (pun not intended), as very little is actually known about the Eraser, and as such there is little data with which to make comparisons.

The previously undisclosed prelude to this expedition began just a few short years after the Erasure. The field technician found a half-burnt diary of Alexander von Humboldt under a floorboard in a home he inherited when his family perished in the Erasure. He shared it with a dear friend (the ethnoarcheologist), who then analyzed Humboldt's scribbled notes and drawings and, combined with a study of mytholog-ical depictions of humanity-destroying organic beings and a discourse analysis of shipping reports from ancient Caribbean sailors and pirates, determined that the creature was most likely a cephalopod. She then involved the teuthologist, who, in collaboration with the hydrologist, determined that the erasure of all non-frozen water on the planet could have in fact been caused by the mating of two megacolossal cepha-lopods. At this point the team started calling them the Erasers. The team enlisted a volcanologist and an aviator and set out from Basseterre. Having visited the sites of other famous cavecanems in the region, the volcanologist was able to determine the maximum height of the Eraser (4,500 meters). The teuthologist determined that the living Eraser, who is hypothesized to have killed the other Eraser in the mating process, could be able to spit ink or some other substance an additional 5,000 meters. As a result, the aviator was instructed to fly at an altitude of at least 10,000 meters as the plane approached the Gran Roque Cavecanem.

The first thing that the team observed upon reaching the Los Roques Archipelago was that, unlike the other cavecanems, the Gran Roque Cavecanem was filled with clear, beautiful water, which appeared to be boiling due to the heat of the burning salt within the cavecanem. The team had anticipated this, and accordingly the aviator had been given a triple ration of water. Otherwise, he could have been tempted to fly the plane straight for the pool. The aviator then, as planned, launched a missile into the water of the Gran Roque Cavecanem. The missile's collision with the bubbling water caused the faintest of ripples, and that minor undulation was enough to send the rest of the team to near frenzy. However, the bursting forth of an utterly massive tentacle was enough to distract them from their thirst.

Though the field team had been anticipating some kind of massive creature, the sight of a kilometer-long tentacle flying upward toward the plane was almost too much to comprehend.

After an expert maneuver by the aviator, the team watched with panicked breath to see if the Eraser would rise for further attack. However, it did not; perhaps it is so sated from its destruction of humanity that it has grown complacent. The hydrologist regained her composure and began to study temperatures and density readings off of her sonar-based system.

The aviator, as instructed, kept his eyes on the horizon, making wide circles above the cavecanem but not looking at the Eraser as it bathed in its boiling layer. At first, the creature was still camouflaged, wearing the color of the burning, wet walls around it: a bright, hot orange. This had allowed it to remain unseen by the post-Erasure aerial explorations commissioned by leadership. But as the plane circled, the beast transformed into a greenish black before shifting back to orange. Its head resembled a massive, two-kilometer-wide cuttlefish.

Finally, the hydrologist said, "I found it," in a reverential whisper and the entire team roared in approval. The hydrologist had found the location of the other Eraser's corpse, which she has hypothesized may contain the fertilized Eraser eggs we believe to be responsible for the Erasure.

As if it had heard the team's cheers, the Eraser rolled its head upward and opened its many eyes, which covered its entire head. Hundreds of house-sized, blank grey circles with comparatively tiny linear red pupils stared up at the aircraft with distant regard.

The field technician must note that the creature, murderer of billions, was simultaneously the most repulsive and beautiful thing he had ever seen. It was a shock to the entire team to see that it appeared to be very much an animal and therefore undeserving of their hatred.

—*E. Humbletrot*

El Avila National Park
10.5833° N, 66.5833° W

HUMBOLDT NOTES:
I am convinced that our happiness or unhappiness depends more on the way we meet the events of life than on the nature of those events themselves.

—*A. Humboldt*

FIELD NOTES:
The view from the ruins of the Humboldt Hotel is quite spectacular. One can see for miles, particularly as the lack of water has made the weather rather inactive and the lack of industry has left the air quite clear.

The hotel was named for the field technician's ancestor and sits atop Mount Avila, providing the spectacular view. From the skeleton of the hotel's cliffside veranda one can peer down at what used to be Caracas or in the opposite direction into the great, salty off-white expanse of what was once the Caribbean Sea.

The field technician and the rest of the team have set up camp at the Humboldt Hotel for the final part of this noble expedition. From here, it is possible to observe the Eraser from the relatively safe distance of 150 kilometers. While the creature could reach us in a matter of seconds, having left its subterranean nest to lurch, arachnid-like, upon the desolate surface of what used to be the island of Fransisqui, the team has hypothesized that it will not leave its eggs.

The team will return to Basseterre after a period of proper observation of the Eraser, in order to ensure that the disturbance of the creature hasn't agitated it to the point of further global catastrophe.

The team's return will be notable for more than just the companionship of a chicken-sized, salt-eating jungle bird, though Nightbird deserves to be welcomed with the effervescent mixture of hope and joy that humanity misplaced long ago. Whether or not vengeance or even progress results from the field team's discoveries, this noble expedition will have been a success. The team returns with the knowledge that the Erasure was committed by force rather than by fluke. The aim of returning time to humankind may also be realized, as knowledge of the beast that nearly destroyed humanity may allow for its sterilization or (though hope to this degree may be inappropriate) destruction. Either result would give humans time. Time to rebuild, time to repossess, time to renew.

The field technician's ancestor observed that human happiness is determined by how obstacles are met, rather than the obstacles themselves (the field technician must note that he is paraphrasing). The information gathered on this expedition will allow humanity to meet the catastrophic events of the Erasure, mysterious for so long, with knowledge and action.

—E. Humbletrot

Cannibal Acts

Maureen McHugh

THERE'S A DIFFERENCE between dissection and butchering. Dissection reveals, but butchering renders. I'm a dissector, professionally, pressed into service as a butcher. I mean, I was a biologist. Am a biologist.

The body in front of me is a man. I know him, although not very well—there aren't that many of us so I know pretty much everybody. His name is Art. He looks much smaller, positively shrunken, laid out in the kitchen, and very, very white. I haven't seen many naked male bodies but I am intimately acquainted with Art's. I have washed him. I'm not attracted to men when they're alive, much less when they're dead, but I feel a weird protectiveness toward Art. I've felt the soft spot in his skull from the fall that killed him. I have washed around his balls and the curled mushroom of his penis. I have cradled his hard and bony feet.

Now I tie a rope around his ankles and hoist him. This is a commercial kitchen with big steel counters and a Hobart dishwasher. The pulley in the ceiling is new. It sounds easy—"I tie a rope around his ankles and hoist him"—but I am not very strong these days and just one pulley means I'm hauling his whole weight. I don't know what Art weighs. He used to weigh more; we all used to weigh more. I am so tired, my fingers are cold. I'm seeing spots when I pull hard on the rope.

Kate has taken to calling the town Leningrad, which is lost on most of the people here. It's because we're under siege in this stupid little Alaska excuse. It's got an airstrip, a Coast Guard base, an Army listening post, a dozen houses, and it's surrounded on two sides by water—the ocean at our back and a river called Pilot's Creek on one side. The Army listening post was monitoring the Russians, of course, which is probably where Kate got the idea of Leningrad.

So anyway, I get Art hanging, fingers just sweeping the floor. The dead are limp. Heavy. One of the locals used to hunt when there was anything to hunt. Eric Swetzof is a long-bodied, short-legged native Unagan. Maybe, he says, he and his wife are the last Unagan left alive. He told me the steps to field dressing a large animal.

Eric is not going to eat Art. There is a group of people who have declared themselves to be non-eaters. Eric says he understands the people who have voted to eat and he doesn't judge them, he just can't. Can't cross that line.

I understand him, too. I stand in front of a human with a good knife. "Blade at least four inches long," Eric said. "You want a real handle on the thing, and a guard. When the knife hits bone it can turn and you can end up cutting yourself."

I used to like to cook. I've cut chickens into parts. I'm familiar with the way a joint shines white with ligament and tendon. What hangs in front of me is an animal. I am an animal. I don't believe there is something particularly special about bodies and I don't believe in souls, the afterlife, or the resurrection of the dead. I tell myself that this is a technical challenge. It's a skill I have some parts of and I will learn the rest as I go.

I am not sentimental.

I put a plastic tub underneath Art to catch blood and viscera.
It's still very hard to open his throat. His viscera are lukewarm.
I'm so hungry.

BUTCHERING HAS GOTTEN ME out of manning the defenses today. We
all have to man the defenses but I'm nearsighted and terrible with a gun.
Luckily, there isn't much shooting because neither side has much in the
way of ammunition. They are mostly men, as best we can tell, a lot of
them fairly young. Maybe thirty of them, some still in ragged military
fatigues. They are in the sharp green hills, waiting us out. They have a
couple of boats, Zodiacs, but we sunk one when they first attacked and
now they either don't want to risk them or they are holding them until
we're too weak to fight back.

Or maybe they're getting too weak to fight.

I find Kate on Beach Road. It runs along the beach, of course, and
then turns inland and runs to the airstrip. It's cloudy and soft, it rains all
summer here. The air off the water smells wrong. It should smell of fish
and salt, that slightly rank and pleasant stink of ocean, but instead there's
a taste to it, like nail polish or something. Organics. Esters and aldehydes.

Kate is sitting cross-legged with a paperback on one knee and a
rifle next to her. Technically she's on sentry, watching the ocean, but
we're sloppy civilians. Does the distinction even matter anymore? She's
taller than me—a lot of people are taller than me. I'm 5'4". She's rangy;
a long-legged, raw-boned woman with large hands and feet. She's originally from New Mexico but she's an Anglo with light hair and blue eyes.

I am still surprised when I see her in glasses. She has worn contacts
as long as I have known her. She was always going to get corrective eye
surgery. Too late now.

McHugh

I can't tell if she is pleased to see me. I mean, usually she would be, but she knows what I've been doing. Kate is a non-eater.

I sit down next to her and watch the chop.

"All done?" she asks.

I nod.

I think for a moment she is going to ask me if I'm OK, which is something we would have done for each other before. She doesn't and I don't know what I would answer if she did. I'm both not OK and weirdly OK.

"What's the book?" I ask.

She flips it over so I can see the cover. *The Da Vinci Code*. I can't help it, I bark out a laugh. Kate hated the book when it came out.

She sighs. "There aren't that many books here at the end of the world."

"It's not the end of the world," I snap.

She rolls her eyes. "Don't tell me about the Great Oxygenation Event or Snowball Earth again or I'll scream."

It isn't the end of the world—just maybe the end of us. Or maybe not, humans are clever beasts and the world is a big place. It's probably not even the biggest extinction event the Earth has ever seen. The Permian extinction killed something like 95 percent of life—including bacteria. Life comes back. It may take millions of years. First bacteria, then multicellular organisms, then plants and animals. We're just another set of dinosaurs, about to go extinct. Although some dinosaurs actually survived the Cretaceous-Tertiary extinction. We just call them birds.

"You're sitting there composing a speech," Kate says.

"I'm not going to say anything," I say.

"You intellectualize as a defense mechanism."

"I don't think psychologists talk about defense mechanisms anymore," I say. Back when we were both at the university we were also both in therapy. Growing up gay pretty much ensured you were messed up about something. My therapist told me I was an emotophobe—afraid of negative emotions.

"What's your defense mechanism?" I ask.

She laughs. "These days? Anger. When I have the energy."

I brought her here. Not specifically here, this ass-end little Alaskan town, but "here" as in leaping at a chance to go to Juneau to study giant viruses and get us away from the increasing chaos of the lower forty-eight.

I look at her wrists, narrow, the knob of the styloid process standing under scaly skin. Her ankles are swollen.

Kate and I bitched about Houston the entire time we lived there. When I took the position, I had no idea that Houston was tropical. Ninety-eight degrees in the summer with ninety-nine percent humidity. Flying cockroaches the size of my thumb. Getting into the car at the end of the work day was like climbing into a pizza oven.

Honestly, though, I remember Houston this way:

In the last year we were there, crime was getting horrible. There were refugee camps outside Brownsville and Laredo. Rolling brownouts. We had a used Prius, which was good because gas was rationed. Hamburger was twenty-two dollars a pound.

Kate gardened and we had half a dozen chickens. We had close friends, Ted and Esteban, and we'd take eggs and garden vegetables over to their place and make dinner. They had huge trees in their backyard and a pool. The electricity would go out and we'd sit in the dark and complain about mosquitos and drink beer.

I was coming home from work one day and stopped at a stoplight, as one does, and someone wrenched open the driver's-side door of the Prius. It was a very angry man with a blue bandanna covering half of his face. He'd have looked like some kind of old movie bandit if he hadn't also been wearing sunglasses. He was waving around a gun and screaming at me.

He yelled "Get out of the car!" at some point.

Back in the day, if you were on Facebook or Tumblr, and you were a woman, you probably got safety tips in your feed. I had read *something* about whether you were safer in a car or out of it although I think it was about getting into a car with someone who was armed—like someone who was going to get you into the car and take you somewhere. I remember it seemed vitally important to know whether I was safer in the car or out of it but I couldn't remember and in the end I scooted across the middle console and out the passenger's-side door.

He got in the car and drove off. My laptop was in the back seat. I had the key fob in my pocket, so he didn't have that.

The police came and we went down to the police station and I told them everything. Then Kate took me home in a Lyft and Esteban made me a precious vodka martini (vodka was expensive) and everyone came over and sat around, commiserating. The electricity went out and we lit a couple of candles. I remember people brought food. Ted said he could take me to work the next day. Another neighbor volunteered to pick me up at work—it wasn't that far out of her way.

I was genuinely shaken. I don't want you to think that I wasn't. But it was such a pleasure to be the center of everyone's concern and attention. As the city vibrated into pieces around our ears, we worked to take care of each other.

In Houston I was studying big viruses. Everyone was, all over the country. My head of research, an asshole named Mark Adams, said it was like the nineties when everybody got sucked into the Human Genome Project. Careers were stagnant for a decade, he said.

Careers. Imagine worrying about a career.

Imagine having deep discussions about things at conferences in Atlanta or Baltimore. Big viruses were different from regular viruses. They didn't just take over a cell and destroy it to make new viruses. They took over a cell and turned it into a virus factory, pumping out viruses at an order of magnitude higher. They had already been linked with a meningitis outbreak in India.

I was doing work on ATP, the energy transfer mechanism in cells, and how the virus co-opted the system. I was at a conference and ended up sitting next to a guy named Zhou Limin from the University of Science and Technology of China in Hefei. We'd corresponded but never met.

We ended up getting lunch. He was a short, intense guy in glasses. He'd done graduate work at Penn State and been a post doc at UCLA so he spoke great English. We bitched about the emphasis on virus coatings and how that was a legacy of HIV research and how the organizers of the conference were biased toward those people.

"You want a beer?" he asked.

I didn't know if he knew I'm gay. I think I did the thing where I said I had promised to call and check in with my girlfriend.

He didn't care so we ended up sitting in the hotel bar, some Hilton or Sheraton. The beers were nineteen dollars a piece.

"Let me expense it," he said.

"USTC covers alcohol?" I asked.

He grinned. "There'd be mutiny if they didn't."

Sometimes I fantasized about doing work in China. There were fewer restrictions there. The Chinese were willing to play fast and loose with ethics. I mean, I knew it would not really be anything like I thought; their office politics were complicated and so were their governmental. "I wish we could do some of the things you guys can do," I said.

He turned his beer glass in his hands. "The government is weaponizing big viruses," he said. "They're trying to make them to deliver bird flu."

Everyone talked about what China might be doing. China had been the first country to bring human clones to term in violation of international ethics. Of course we thought they might do something like this. "You know for sure?" I asked.

"I know people on the project," he said. "I've seen some of the results."

so, you might think I would instantly rush to the government or to the newspapers. That I was in a position to save the world.

But I wasn't. What were we going to do, invade China over microbiology? All that would happen was that Zhou would be compromised. I think he just had to tell somebody and I was the stranger on a plane.

I told a couple friends without mentioning Zhou. Then I saw the job listing at a new lab in Juneau and it sounded so far away, so clean and cold and safe. (Juneau was actually like Seattle, wet and green.) I remember watching TV in the airport while we waited to catch our plane first to Salt Lake City and then to Seattle and then on to Alaska. There were reports on the bird flu epidemic in Russia. Russia had been saber rattling at China in Mongolia and the Chinese had retaliated. In a month we were all working on ways to stop the viruses—vaccinations, antivirals, manufactured viruses that spread their own antivirus (and look how well that went in Japan). People were getting sick all over the world. Kate got sick early on and was in the hospital on a ventilator for three days. She was lucky. In a month there were nowhere near enough ventilators for the people who needed them and infection among hospital staff was running at over 80 percent.

Pakistan and India went to war and we all waited for India to drop the bomb, but instead North Korea nuked Tianjin and Los Angeles.

The pandemic was burning unchecked—bird flu, the counterflu—and it seemed like being near other people was a terrible idea. We decided to retreat to a cabin on the Alaska Peninsula. It was owned by a guy in my department but he was dead.

My parents died in the pandemic. Kate's mother, too. We don't know about her father, she hadn't talked to him in a decade. Is Houston still there?

It's like asking if Troy is still there. There's a place on the map marked Troy but nobody has lived in those ruins or called it Troy in millenia. Maybe someone still lives in Houston. Maybe Ted is standing on his back deck looking at his empty swimming pool and he's converted it into a kind of greenhouse, like he always threatened. Maybe they are growing things. Maybe the chickens we gave him live there.

Everything we try to grow here in Alaska dies and no one, least of all me, knows what that means.

IN THE LATE AFTERNOON there are gunshots and I scramble to the airstrip. Scramble is a relative term. When I stand up too quickly, I see spots. We all conserve energy. But the rule is, when you hear shots, anyone not on sentry has to grab a weapon and go.

We dug trenches and put up barricades of useless vehicles, trash, and fence before these guys even showed up. I find Eric. The big man is crouched in a trench.

"What's the password," he says. A joke between us.

"Leningrad," I say. "Where's Deb?" Deb's his wife.

He shrugs. Eric doesn't talk much. It took me a long time to figure out he's a sarcastic bastard. He's so deadpan it's scary.

"What are they doing?" I ask. "I heard shots."

(I wish I could say I was some sort of intrepid survivor, but the first time someone shot at me I just froze. I hunkered down and couldn't move. Eric's comment later was, "It happens.")

"They aren't doing anything," Eric says.

I watch the green and granite hills. No sign of movement in their trenches.

"I wonder how much food they've got," I say. "Maybe we should do some kind of nighttime sneak attack." Not that there's much night at this time of year.

"Jeff said no," Eric says. Jeff is our elected mayor/commandant.

I'm tired from jogging to the airstrip and these days my concentration is pretty shot so I sit for a minute carefully studying the landscape and feeling empty and stupid. (And thinking about Art cooking back in the kitchen.) "Wait, you suggested it?"

Eric glances at me, expressionless, which I think is Eric speak for "Are you a moron?" He looks back out at the blank hills.

We sit there for a while and I try to figure out what that means. It starts to drizzle.

"Do you think they're planning something?" I ask.

"I think they're desperate," Eric says.

"Join the club," I say.

Eric looks at me, stonefaced. But I'm beginning to get when he's amused. I think he's amused.

THE EATERS ASSEMBLE in the canteen. Len did the cooking. He has worked very hard to make sure that Art no longer looks like Art. We have Art a couple of ways. We have some of Art roasted and sliced thin. Lean strips of meat. The rest is boiled. So here it is: human flesh tastes . . . pretty bland. Tough and maybe a little bitter. I can see why people compare it to veal or pork or chicken. I am so hungry but I eat it slowly. Len cries as he eats. He was a fisherman—like the guys in the television show who catch crab, only he worked on boats that caught halibut, pollock, and herring and occasionally did stints in processing plants. I almost sat down next to him, solidarity in our grisly parts in this meal. But I thought maybe it was better if I didn't make us so obvious.

There isn't a lot of meat. The broth is salty. I feel full.

Thank you, Art.

I wonder who at this table will eat me? Although I'm a short woman and there's a good chance I'll outlive most of the men.

I almost fall asleep at the table. Spoons clink against bowls. Len cries as he drinks spoonfuls, salty tears slipping into his ragged beard, flannel shirt loose on him.

A SINGLE GUNSHOT the next morning brings us to the airstrip.

It's sunny for a change. Kate and I walk over together. We haven't said anything about what I've done. It should have been some kind of personal Rubicon and maybe it was but what I feel is that I held out on Kate. That I didn't share food with her. Like I cheated. There was a time when we'd have talked about it. It's what lesbians do, you know, we talk and talk. We negotiate our needs and our wants. We explore our feelings. But here, at the end of the world, it's okay that some things won't be resolved. We'll go to our deaths with resentments and unfairness clutched to us like greedy children. What else have we got?

There's a white T-shirt flying on a stick.

We all sit on the ground, the edge of a trench, whatever. I mostly feel as if I don't have the energy to deal with this. Not after Art. No more decisions.

"What do you want to do?" Len asks everybody and nobody in particular.

"They surrendering?" Callie asks.

Eric's face doesn't exactly change but I suspect he's thinking, "moron."

Callie is perfectly nice. I think she was local, administration. Like a secretary or data entry. I can imagine her thinking she'd work for a few years, get a nest egg, and then get a job in Juneau. Or maybe she's like a lot of Alaskans and she likes the ass end of nowhere and she had a husband who loved snowmobiles or something.

"I don't trust them," she says.

Oh for Christ's sake.

"We can ask them," I say. I thought I was too worn down to care but I remain myself—opinionated and unwilling to shut up till the end.

Everyone looks at me.

I stand up and yell over the tipped Land Cruiser that forms part of a barricade. I yell, "Hey! Are you surrendering?"

Kate finds me embarrassing sometimes.

A guy comes over the hill. He's dressed in camo pants and a T-shirt and he looks normal, not super skinny. He waves his arms. "We need help! We're dying! We're sick!"

"All of you come out in the open!" Eric yells.

It's a long five minutes or so before three men shuffle to the edge of the airstrip. We shout back and forth. They are all that's left, they say. We don't believe them. One of them weeps.

It takes most of the morning before we are convinced. There are four more guys too sick to walk. We could shoot them.

They don't look starving. That's the important thing.

"What if we quarantine them?" Kate asks me.

"We'd be talking Ebola levels of decontamination," I say. "Bleach. The whole nine yards. We don't have that stuff."

"I've already had the flu," she points out. "I'd be immune. I'd just have to be very careful."

Three of us have had it and survived. They decide to risk meeting; everyone else will be ready for an ambush. We have rubber boots and

Wellingtons, and latex gloves and hairnets that were for the kitchen staff. The three put on raincoats and gear and I use duct tape to seal the sleeves of the raincoats to the tops of the latex gloves. When they come back I will make them walk through tubs of bleach and wash everything off before putting on a pair of gloves and taking all the homemade gear off.

"Cover me," Kate says to me, grinning—I am a terrible shot—and walks across the airstrip.

No one shoots.

That evening, in our bed, she tells me what it was like. The graves. The newly dead. The smell. The sick. The trash and carelessness. "They were, like, teenagers," she says. One of the sick men died during the afternoon.

There is a box truck three-quarters full of supplies. Bags of beans and rice. MREs. These weird emergency bars.

Kate tells me they were convinced we had medical supplies. One of them said that he knew we had supplies when they smelled meat cooking. They assumed then that we had power, maybe a freezer.

"They're just kids," she says. "Like my students." Kate taught English, Freshman Composition, in Houston. "Just clueless kids."

"Like we have a clue," I say.

We eat MREs. Mine is Mexican chicken stew. There is the stew and a packet of red pepper to spice it up, Spanish-style rice, and jalapeño nacho cheese spread. There are cheese-filled pretzel nuggets. There is Hawaiian punch, so sugary that when I taste it, tears come to my eyes. And these weird crackers, like saltines but coarser. Some weird refried beans with so much flavor. There's a full-sized bag of peanut M&M's. It's weird, seeing it all bright. It's exotic.

Kate gets spaghetti with meat sauce (we reached in and drew blind so we wouldn't know what we were getting). We agree she won. It's like canned spaghetti and comes with a weird cracker that is shaped like a slice of bread but isn't either bread or a cracker. Cheez Whiz–type stuff, hot sauce, potato sticks, and blueberry-cherry cobbler.

I feed her some of mine because, I keep saying, I ate yesterday. Besides, I'm full. We share her blueberry-cherry cobbler, which has no crust and isn't really anything like a cobbler but who cares and we keep the M&M's to share in bed.

Cheese and crackers! A meal!

It makes me think that maybe we'll survive. Maybe in a few months there will be fish in the ocean and Len will show us ways to catch them. It makes me think that a society that made things this marvelous will not just disappear.

It makes me think that none of the rest of us will get the flu.

It makes me believe we will hang on.

We sit in our bed in the big main building of the Coast Guard station—no one lives in the houses because they are too hard to defend. Our home is a mattress and box spring sitting on the floor of an office, next to a desk. I feed Kate a yellow M&M and eat a brown one.

"Don't eat all the brown ones," she says.

"Oh, do you like them best?"

"No, you're giving me all the pretty ones and eating all the broken and brown ones."

"I ate yesterday," I say.

"I ate today." She picks up a red one and holds it out to me on the palm of her hand.

I take it.

"I'm sorry," I say. "I'm sorry I ate." I wish they had surrendered before.

"I want you to eat," she says.

"You're not."

"I am," she says, and pops an M&M in her mouth. "Now I am again."

I sigh and settle on my side.

"Promise me you'll eat me," she says. "If it happens."

I don't say anything.

"You're so brave," she whispers. "I would if I could but I can't. I can't be like you."

I smell the M&M's and the dusty carpet. I feel the bones of my hips on the mattress.

"Eat me because I love you," she says. "Because you love me. Because you have to. Promise me."

Waving at Trains

Nalo Hopkinson

SUMMERS, Priithi and I were on our own while our parents were at work. We would meet in the corner of the playground, by that big old tamarind tree; you know the one? When it was close to tamarind season, and the fruit green and hard on the tree, the boys from the boys' school across the way would pick the unripe tamarind pods and pelt the girls from our school with them, till the caretaker came and shooed them away. By the time summer holidays came around, any fruit left on the tree would ripen, getting fat and brown. Then they would just fall to the ground, cracking their brittle shells open when they landed. Ants and mongoose would feed on the broken fruit.

Today the tropical sun was beating down warm on my head—Priithi would scold me for not wearing my hat—and my sandals kicked up grey dirt with each step, powdering my bare legs almost to the knee. I stopped to pull the belt tighter around the waistband of the khaki shorts I was wearing. They were my brother's, way too big for me. The pockets sagged and the hems came almost to my knees. But Priithi said khaki would be better for walking and climbing in than my light sundresses, and along with the brown T-shirt I was wearing, I would be harder to spot when we got into the bush. She said all those bright flower patterns I liked to wear wouldn't be any good. She was probably right. Too besides, those big pockets would be good for carrying pelting stones in, and the pocket knife I had found in the back of a kitchen drawer at home.

Something must be was dead in the underbrush by the side of the road. At first, the back of my neck went cold. But then I realized that the rotten smell had a cooked quality to it, like when you drop an egg into a frying pan with hot oil in it before you realize that the egg spoil. Whatever was hidden by the crackly, dried-up scrub over there, it wasn't moving anymore.

Still. No cars on the road, so I moved away from the roadside and walked along the broken white line down the middle. Made me feel deliciously wicked. If Daddy could see me, he would trace me off for walking in the road like that.

Daddy couldn't see me.

My throat was parched. I hoped Priithi had brought some water from the standpipe in her yard. The taps in our house weren't working.

When we had nothing else to do on those summer days, Priithi and I would go down to the train tracks and wait for passenger trains to pass. We'd wave at the people inside. Our hearts leapt when anyone waved back. It was as though, by them opening a hand to us, they were taking a little piece of us with them to wherever they were going, to exciting places we couldn't travel to.

The trains weren't coming right now, though.

Priithi was waiting for me by the gate to the playground. "You have everything?" she asked.

"For our hike? Yeah." I pointed to the rucksack on my back.

She craned her neck to look behind me. "Look like you scarcely fill it at all, Angela."

My face got hot, hotter than the sunshine warming it. "I did! I put in everything you said!"

"You put the matches?"

"Yes, but I only find half a box."

"Not even a lighter?"

I was so stupid. "I didn't think of that." Mummy kept a lighter in her purse. I should have gotten it out of there. It would only have been a little messy. "You want us to go back and get it?" I certainly wasn't going to go alone.

"Never mind," Priithi said. "We will manage."

"You bring water, Priithi? I so thirsty!"

She cut her eyes at me. "Of course not. You know you have to come and help me with it."

She was right. Water was heavy to carry, and we would need plenty of it for the two of us. "But I don't want to go to your house," I said.

"Coward."

"I just don't want to see . . ."

"It not so bad," she replied. "Mostly dried up."

I took a deep, shaky breath and turned in the direction of Priithi's place. And, once again, she was right. The school was quiet, but then, people had stopped going there when it all started. The cows lying in the field across from the sweetie shop were like big raisins. There weren't as many flies buzzing around outside the shop, like before. So I guessed Mrs. Kramer who owned the shop was in the same shape as the cows. The people in the few cars along the roadside were quiet and still. Even Mummy had been almost dried up. I could have pried her hand off her handbag easy to get her lighter. I should have realized when I smelled the something dead in the weeds; it was happening all over town. For the past month, everything had smelled like that, everywhere. The first symptom was dehydration. Then would come fever, bellyache, attacking people, then getting quiet, lying down, deading, and drying up and floating away on the wind.

Priithi and I were going to walk our way out of town. In my rucksack, I had some stale bread, a can of condensed milk, and a roll of toilet paper. We would only need one, don't it? We wouldn't get very far. Don't someone would come and rescue us soon?

The sun was so hot! I rubbed my belly. I was getting vex. At everything, at everyone. Except Priithi.

If I concentrated really hard, I could feel Priithi's hand on my shoulder, guiding me to her house.

There was a rat lying by the roadside. Its legs were still moving a little bit. Something exploded in my mind. Screaming, I stomped it into pulp. The squishing and crunching under my sandals was almost as good as drinking cool water on a hot day. I scraped my sandals off along the ground and headed toward Priithi's place again.

It would be all right. When I got there, I just wouldn't look at her. I would just get some water from the standpipe; I was so parched! Then maybe I would lie down for a little rest before I walked away from this town.

Interviews & Essays

Make Margaret Atwood Fiction Again

Margaret Atwood interviewed by Junot Díaz

Margaret Atwood's award-winning dystopian novel, *The Handmaid's Tale*, was published in 1985 to critical and popular success. The novel is set in a near-future in which right-wing fundamentalists overthrow the United States government and set up the Republic of Gilead in its place. Gilead is a totalitarian and theocratic state in which fertile women are kept in sexual slavery as Handmaids and forced to bear children for infertile couples.

JUNOT DÍAZ: "Make Margaret Atwood Fiction Again" was a phrase used on many signs in January's Women's March, highlighting that a lot of people feel life under Trump is a dystopia for women. Do you feel that way?

MARGARET ATWOOD: Yes. I'm in Canada but, as you know, I lived in the States for some years and have a lot of friends there. It's not only

Trump. The general climate in some parts of the United States is certainly heading in a *Handmaid's Tale* direction. And that is why the recent sit-ins in state legislatures were so immediately understandable, with groups of women in "Handmaid" costumes turning up, for instance, in Texas, while an all-male batch of lawmakers were passing laws on women's health issues. They just sat there, they didn't say anything, so they couldn't be ejected, and there was a very telling photograph of them surrounded by men with guns, which could have been right out of the Hulu television adaptation of *The Handmaid's Tale*.

JD: So our society is in many ways doing a better job of reenacting the book than one would have imagined possible.

MA: Much more than one would have imagined. In 1985 it was only a possibility. In some places in the United States today, it's approaching reality. And as you know, I put nothing into the book that people had not done at some time, in some place. And in some countries in the world, these are pretty much the realities now.

JD: I read *The Handmaid's Tale* when it was first published, and despite the rapid rise of the religious right and its effort to roll back reproductive rights in that decade, the world in the book still felt distant. Are you struck by how, for those who are just coming to the book now, reading it is a very different experience?

MA: It is quite different now. There were national differences at the time of publication. In England it was viewed as a jolly good yarn, but they didn't think of Gilead as something that was going to happen to them, because they did their religious warfare in the seventeenth century and had lived through a lot of other bad stuff that they thought they had gotten over—although, in recent days, apparently not. In Canada it was the usual worried Canadian question—"Could it happen here?"—though I didn't have to explain to Canadians why my characters were escaping to Canada, because we have been escaped to quite a lot in history. But in the United States, particularly on the West Coast, they said—somebody spray-painted on the Venice Beach seawall—"*The Handmaid's Tale* is already here." That was in 1985.

Some people mistakenly thought that the book was somehow anti-Christian. That's not the case that is being made. Some Christians would resist such a regime, and do in the book. Others would be eliminated by the regime, because they would be the competition. And others would use religion as an excuse for what they're doing—which has certainly happened a lot in history too, with all sorts of religions.

JD: When I recall the novel's reception in the eighties, there was a lot of turmoil around the question of whether the novel was too hard on fundamentalist Christians. And yet, now, of course, that criticism has fallen away, and it seems to me that what was most frightening about the novel is only now coming to the foreground.

It also seems there's more space to talk about the state-sanctioned rape that the novel portrays than there was in the mid-eighties.

MA: Oh, for sure. Well, part of the exploration is, if you want to take the Bible literally, how literally do you want to take it? Which parts are you going to be "literal" about? The Bible is an amazingly compendious book, and people have been foregrounding parts of it and backgrounding other parts since forever. But if you want to take the text literally—polygamy and using "handmaids" as surrogate mothers despite anything they might have to say about it—it's right there. Joseph and his two wives, Rachel and Leah, and their two handmaids; amongst the four women they have twelve sons, but the wives claim the handmaids' babies, which is why I put an excerpt from Genesis at the front of the book, and why I called the training place for Handmaids the Rachel and Leah Center. It's very literal.

But the real question is, if the United States were going to have totalitarianism, what kind of totalitarianism would it be? We've had all kinds in the world, including atheist ones. But if the United States were ever going to go down that path, what would be the device under which it would do it? It certainly would not be communism.

JD: I think that's very true. You've said before that Gilead already exists at low levels in many places.

MA: No kidding. And sometimes at pretty high levels too. There are thirteen countries in the world in which homosexuality is punishable by death.

JD: Yes. That's another element of the novel that I think is even more resonant today than it was in the mid-eighties. You have what we might call the "long view." Do these times we're living in feel particularly apocalyptic? In your life, what other dark periods do these times recall?

MA: Well, since I was born in 1939, two months after World War II began, of course I was immersed in news about totalitarianism growing up—Nazis, Benito Mussolini, Joseph Stalin, followed by Mao Zedong. And then we've had more than a couple since that time, such as Cambodia under Pol Pot, and Romania, where Nicolae Ceaușescu mandated four children per woman, whether the woman could afford those children or not, and you had to have a fertility test every month, and if you weren't pregnant, you had to say why. What was the result? A lot of orphanages, a lot of neglected children, and a lot of dead women. So if the United States wants to go in that direction, how will it prepare for the results? Is that what it wants, orphans, dead women, and so forth?

Then there's child-stealing—again, I put nothing in the book that people have not done—there have been so many instances of that throughout history. Amongst them, Hitler stole 12,000 blond Polish children and placed them with German families, hoping they would turn into blond German children. And he had the Lebensborn program for SS families, in which unmarried women produced children for them. And of course in Argentina, under the generals—where they were dropping people out of planes—if you were pregnant, they didn't drop you out of a plane or otherwise kill you until you had the baby, and then they placed the child with a high-ranking junta family. And the fallout now is that some of the children grew up and then found out the truth about their background.

JD: Listening to that tour of hell that you just gave, one thing that's really striking, and that recalls the Gilead regime, is the centrality of children. That, yes, we've got these enemies of the state whom we're going to torture to death, but they do have these children who are a very valuable resource.

MA: That's right. Gilead, of course, is arranged as a true totalitarianism, where the people at the top get the good stuff. Children are seen as the good stuff, due to their rarity.

JD: In your novel, one of the ways that Gilead defines who is "other" is through race, and it dispatches the non-white with Nazi precision.

MA: They are put into closed "homelands." As in apartheid South Africa.

JD: It has been remarked that the Hulu adaptation mutes this.

MA: Hulu updated the time period of the "before" part of the show to now. In 1985 it was much more plausible that you might be able to carry out that kind of resegregation.

JD: To round up all the folks of color.

MA: Yes. But the television version—which gave us Samira Wiley as Moira, for which we are grateful—takes the view that there are, at the present time, many more interracial friendships and relationships than there would have been in 1985. Which is true. And Bruce Miller, the showrunner, said, in essence, who wants to watch a show that's all white people? Not to mention that Hulu has a general policy of diversity. We also both felt that in Gilead—the modern television version—fertility would rank higher than racialization as a way of categorizing people and deciding who gets what treatment.

JD: Women in the homelands or "Colonies," if they are difficult (to use a euphemism), get sent to the secret Gilead brothel of the Jezebels.

MA: I would contend that it might be easier to escape from Jezebels. So, from the point of view of somebody writing the television script, having Moira at Jezebels means there's a chance she could get out. And she has gotten out once before.

JD: I was in Toronto recently and it was a very fascinating time to be there. It was just becoming clear at the time what an explosive success *The Handmaid's Tale* show was going to be. I spent four days there talking to a whole bunch of smart, bright young folks. Kind of the new face of Toronto. And it seems that currently Toronto—and we could say by extension Canada—has two global superstars: Margaret Atwood and Drake. Have you met Drake?

MA: I haven't met Drake, but I have of course met people who have met Drake. But you have to realize how *old* I am. I'm not likely to go to the same parties. Or many parties at all, to be frank.

JD: I understand. I just think that, Canada—I'll say this to the whole nation—you are missing a great opportunity to put these two folks together.

MA: Wouldn't it be fun for him to have a cameo in the second season of *The Handmaid's Tale*? I'll drop that notion into the ear of Miller and see what he can do, because the show is filmed in Toronto. Maybe Drake could help smuggle someone?

JD: It is an extraordinary time. I've never seen young Canadians so thrilled to have these models.

MA: And energized. Toronto is, according to the people who count, the most diverse city in the world.

JD: A lot of these young folks were saying to me that a very Canadian virtue is to be humble, not to dream too big. And I have to say, you have given a lot of young people—you and Drake—new horizons. And it is a wonderful thing to see.

MA: Thank you. You've given me a new idea. Drake in *The Handmaid's Tale*!

Saving Orwell

Peter Ross

"IT WAS A BRIGHT COLD DAY in April," said Richard Blair, "and the clocks were striking thirteen."

Blair is seventy-three and the son of George Orwell. To witness him stand at a lectern and read the opening line of his father's great final novel, *1984*, is to experience a sense of completion, an equation solved.

We were in Senate House, now part of the University of London, for *1984* Live. For the first time in the United Kingdom, the book was to be read aloud publicly from start to finish. It had been estimated that it would take sixty or so readers—well-known journalists, academics, actors, activists—thirteen hours, that Orwellian number, to get from the bright cold day to the gin-scented tears.

The event was being organized by the Orwell Foundation, a charity celebrating the author's work and values. Its director, Jean Seaton, explained that the idea had come "last summer, just after Brexit, but before Trump. The world felt dark and full of lies. Still does."

Since then, *1984* has taken on a strange currency; the electric charge of Orwell's thinking hums and crackles through the culture.

In January the novel topped Amazon's bestseller list, almost seventy years since it was first published in 1949. Demand began to rise, according to Penguin Random House, shortly after Kellyanne Conway used the expression "alternative facts" to defend Sean Spicer's claim that Donald Trump had attracted the largest audience ever to witness a presidential inauguration, *period*. By July 2017 sales had doubled over the same period in 2016. Half a million copies were printed in January alone.

All political moments are Orwellian, but some are more Orwellian than others. Reading *1984* "hurts" right now, according to Jean Seaton, but perhaps there is also something soothing in the recognition that the novel's darkness looks so much like our own. "It feels like *1984* is here in our faces," she told me.

George Orwell, whose real name was Eric Blair, wrote the novel between the summer of 1946 and the winter of 1948, mostly on the island of Jura, off the west coast of Scotland, where he had taken a house, moving there from austere post-war London. It tells the story of Winston Smith, a citizen of the state of Oceania, and his attempted rebellion—through sex and love and the written word—against the Party, which observes and controls every aspect of life. The novel has given us familiar concepts such as Big Brother and Room 101. Published in the United Kingdom on June 8, 1949, and five days later in the United States, the reviews at once recognized its significance. Mark Schorer wrote in the *New York Times* that "no other work of this generation has made us desire freedom more earnestly or loathe tyranny with such fullness."

Orwell grew concerned that the novel was being interpreted across the Atlantic as an anti-communist or anti-left polemic, rather than the warning against totalitarianism that he had intended. True, he said, the name he had given to the political ideology of Oceania was Ingsoc— or English Socialism—but he could easily have chosen something different: "In the USA the phrase 'Americanism' or 'hundred per cent

Americanism' is suitable and . . . as totalitarian as anyone could wish." One thinks of Trump's inauguration, Capitol Hill within a belfry of cloud, and the tolling bell of his promise: "America first, America first."

I HAD WALKED the short distance to Senate House from Euston railway station. Filthy weather, heavy rain, the morning sky a tubercular grey.

Down-and-outs dozed in doorways on Euston Road, nested in flattened boxes, dirty duvets. Old newspapers, spread out upon the cardboard to absorb the rain and cold, were damp and blurred, but some Orwellian headlines were legible: "Terror at London Bridge"; "Massacre in the Market"; "May: Trust Me to Keep You Safe." Photographs showed armed police in black face masks. Three days before, not far from here, eight people were killed and forty-eight injured in a terrorist attack, the third in Britain in just over two months. The Grenfell Tower fire, taking the lives of up to eighty people in a high-rise apartment block, was eight days away from happening, but would—in its ferocious injustice—bring to mind the title of Orwell's 1946 essay "How the Poor Die."

I walked down Gower Street past the red-brick hospital where, on January 21, 1950, Orwell died of a hemorrhage of the left lung, drowning in his own blood. Suddenly, Senate House loomed out of the murk. There could be few more appropriate venues. Orwell took it as his model for the government building where the Party manufactured lies. "The Ministry of Truth," he wrote, "was startlingly different from any other object in sight. It was an enormous pyramidal structure of glittering white concrete, soaring up, terrace after terrace, three hundred meters into the air." In fact Senate House is only sixty-four meters high, although this was enough to make it London's first skyscraper and the tallest secular building in Britain upon its completion in 1936. Evelyn

Ross

Waugh, in his novel *Put Out More Flags* (1942), wrote of its "vast bulk . . . insulting the autumnal sky."

During World War II, Senate House was home to the Ministry of Information, the British government department concerned with propaganda and censorship. Three thousand people worked here, among them Orwell's first wife, Eileen.

Chancellor's Hall, a long narrow room on the first floor of the tower, with marble pillars and a walnut floor, was used during the war by the Home Guard volunteer defense force. According to University of London professor Simon Eliot, "We must imagine this room as a cross between an armory and a command post, with machine guns at the windows, at least one pointing east and one pointing west."

During *1984* Live, the windows of Chancellor's Hall were shuttered, the room lit with cold blue light. The Battle of Britain, the so-called Blitz spirit, seemed a long time ago. Nevertheless, with the terrorism threat level at severe and a general election two days away, there was a mild sense of siege. What, I asked Orwell's biographer D. J. Taylor, did *1984* have to say to us in this moment? Taylor spoke about the novel's attack on those who would limit freedom of thought and expression, and noted that it was, today, being read aloud in a city "scared stiff" of terrorists who hold democracy in contempt. "So," he said, "I would like to think that it is a candle burning on a winter's night."

If so, its flame was brightest at 11:00 a.m. precisely. The journalist Arifa Akbar was at the podium, reading from the section of the book in which Winston Smith, lunching in the Ministry of Truth canteen, listens as his colleague Syme describes, cheerfully, the recent execution of some prisoners. "It was a good hanging," Akbar read. "I think it spoils it when they tie their feet together. I like to see them kicking." Suddenly, there came an announcement. The minute's silence, observed nationwide, in memory of the victims of the attack on London Bridge and Borough Market, was to be held here, too.

The lights were dimmed, heads bowed in the smothering hush. This was the only interruption to *1984* during the whole day, and it felt like part of the book's meaning, a blank page as powerful as anything Orwell had written. Already that morning there had been a reading of the section describing the Two Minutes Hate—a ritualized outpouring of fury at Oceania's enemies. Here, now, was the opposite: a moment of calm reflection with love at its heart. It felt Orwellian in the less common sense of that word: an assertion of the democratic values championed in his work, and the basic human kindness which many of those who knew him say he embodied in life.

Backstage, in the green room, I fell into conversation with Catherine O'Shaughnessy. Orwell was her uncle and godfather. She lives in Virginia, in a small town forty miles south of Washington, D.C. She had come to Europe to take part in this reading and to visit the restored trenches in Aragon where her uncle had fought—and was shot in the neck—during the Spanish Civil War. She knew the man, she said, not the writer. "I remember holding his hand and looking up at him. He was so tall and thin. He just went up and up and up. As a child, it was very easy to be around him."

Orwell was six foot three or four ("up and up and up") with a thirty-seven-inch chest and thirty-three-inch waist. He wore size twelve shoes. His hands were very large with "spatulate" fingers, broad and clublike at the tips, a condition that one close friend regarded as a signifier of his artistic nature, but which can also indicate chronic lung infection. He was gaunt. His eyes were bright blue, and he would look at people in such a direct and penetrating way, a mingled "benevolence and fanaticism," that they remembered it for years afterward. They remembered, too, a certain "luminosity" that he seemed to have, and which photographs have failed to capture. A number of his friends noted a resemblance to Don Quixote. Others compared him to a figure carved on the front of a Gothic cathedral, or a tortured saint by El Greco. There was a "curiously crucified expression," a woodcut melancholy, upon his lined face.

Read deep into the letters, the diaries, the books of reminiscence, and one can glimpse the real man now and then. Illustrated gospels. Scenes from the life. Here is Orwell in 1937 reading Shakespeare in the Spanish trenches. There he is a year later, cross-legged in an English hayfield, laughing at caterpillars. Or sitting up in bed in London, reading *Animal Farm* (1945), then a work-in-progress, to his wife. Or, in 1946, stooping to lift a human skull, some barnacled memento mori, from a beach on Jura; to this favor he would soon come.

This flesh-and-blood Orwell is not well known. He exists more vividly as a set of ideas and moral positions that can be used to shore up one's own argument. Being conveniently dead, he has been pressed into the service of various causes, from invading Afghanistan to remaining part of the European Union. Conservative commentators have described as "Orwellian" the removal of Confederate statues from public space, while liberal pundits have suggested that Antifa—which supports taking down the statues—displays a certain comradeship with Orwell in its willingness to take a physical stand against fascism. There is a tendency by both left and right, as the journalist Paul Gray once wrote, "to hold Orwell's coat while sending his ghost out to battle."

For the Columbia University historian Simon Schama, who had flown to London from New York, *1984*'s continued relevance is illustrated by Orwell's concept of the Ministries of Truth, Love, and Plenty, all of which are concerned with the precise opposite of what their names indicate. For a parallel, he suggested, one need only look to Trump's nomination of Scott Pruitt, a climate change skeptic, to head the

Environmental Protection Agency; or his nomination of Betsy DeVos as education secretary when—as Schama put it—she is the "sworn foe" of public schooling.

"And Trump calling anything he happens to disagree with 'fake news' is *1984* to the letter," he continued. "To take authenticity and evidence and empirically acquired information and stigmatize them as non-truth is just about as Orwellian as you could possibly get."

Not everyone is convinced. "Trump is a horrible oaf, but he's not Big Brother," said the *Mail on Sunday* columnist Peter Hitchens, a former winner of the Orwell Prize for journalism. We were talking in a small exhibition space just along the corridor from Chancellor's Hall; a sign next to the door revealed, almost unbelievably, that this was Room 101.

Hitchens considers "daft" anyone who would respond to Trump's presidency by purchasing *1984*. Why? "Well, you tell me why it would be sensible," he countered. "Donald Trump doesn't threaten a secret police force or surveillance particularly. He doesn't have any ambition to wipe out the past, or impose a new language on people, or police their minds. I just don't see it."

One could argue that he is trying to change the past by lying about it. "Well, yes, but his lies are all discoverable. . . . If people really think that Donald Trump is the worst menace to freedom of speech and thought, and knowledge of the past, then they have to get out a bit more."

Of course, even if one does accept the analogy, where does it get us?

I put this question to singer-songwriter and activist Billy Bragg. "To feel that we're in control . . . we have to have a way of explaining what's happening to us," he replied. "By connecting with Orwell, we realize we're not the first people to have experienced this situation, and we get some comfort from that. Culture can do that for you."

Ross

THE DAY WAS WEARING ON. The readings continued. The story arced ratwards, deathwards. I took some time out and walked down the street to the special collections department of the university library.

There, Gill Furlong, the archivist, led the way down to the windowless basement. White walls. Silver heating pipes. Bright light. A place where there is no darkness.

The partial manuscript of *1984* is at Brown University, but everything else is here: Orwell's diaries, notebooks, some letters, ephemera he brought back from the Spanish Civil War. He stares out from the small black-and-white photo on the front of his press card, faintly amused.

Furlong has worked with these materials since the seventies as their caretaker and guardian, and has developed a sense of intimacy with the man whose relics these are. "I feel very close," she said. "I feel sometimes as though he's standing at my shoulder."

She placed on the desk a hardback notebook, its cover, worn at the edges, the color of red wine. "This notebook is just iconic, isn't it?" she said, opening it toward the back. There, on a right-hand page, Orwell had written and underlined, *The Last Man in Europe*—his original title for *1984*.

A list of words and expressions followed, things he intended to bring into the book. Newspeak. The Two Minutes Hate. And the Party slogans: War Is Peace. Ignorance Is Strength. Freedom Is Slavery.

It was quite a thing to see those words written down in black cursive script. It marks the moment when those ideas, so much part of modern political thought, passed from Orwell's brain to his hand to the page, and from there, eventually, to the world.

The archivist closed the book, fetched another. A green cover, discolored here and there with island-shaped splotches of what looks like rain: Orwell's diary from April to September 1947.

She turned to the entry for August 19. A page from the mythology of Orwell. He describes a trip by dinghy to the western side of the island of Jura. The sea was calm, the weather fine, and then something happened. Furlong read the words out loud: "On return journey today ran into the whirlpool and were all nearly drowned."

The Corryvreckan is the third largest whirlpool in the world. Not only water churns here; stories, too—of sea-hags and drowned Viking princes. It lies in the narrow channel between Jura and the neighboring island of Scarba. Sail into it and its true nature becomes clear: it is not one whirlpool but rather a series of areas where the water seethes and waves butt heads like rutting deer. This unchancy place is where Orwell got into trouble.

In the dinghy with him were his niece Lucie and nephew Henry, as well as his son Richard, who was just three years old. Earlier I had asked Richard whether he had any memory of the accident. "Oh, yes," he had replied. "That's startlingly crisp in my mind." He remembers sitting on his father's knee in the stern, and then the desperate cold of the water.

Orwell had misread the tide tables. He lost control, the outboard motor was torn off the boat, and they were pitched and tossed from one vortex to another. Beside the small uninhabited island of Eilean Mòr, the dinghy overturned. Richard was trapped underneath, but his father pulled him out, and swam with him to the island. After a couple of hours, they were rescued by a passing lobster boat.

Sail past Eilean Mòr—a beautiful striated crag, yellow with lichen and pink with thrift—and one can almost see Orwell marooned there, a slender figure silhouetted against the sun, holding out his clothes to dry as a cormorant holds out its wings.

It is interesting to consider how many times he escaped death: the sniper's bullet, the whirlpool, the blood in his lungs. It was the last that got him eventually, but he held it off for longer than many expected.

Ross

There is a sense of Orwell being saved for a purpose. He had a fond theory—perhaps a kind of prayer—that a writer could not die while he still had a book in him.

ORWELL MADE SEVERAL TRIPS to and from Jura between 1945 and 1949. The island, part of Scotland's Inner Hebrides, is all mountain and moor and loch. At around thirty miles long and seven wide, it is home to a couple of hundred people outnumbered, thirty to one, by red deer. Orwell called it "an extremely un-getatable place"—still true—and valued it as somewhere he could focus on his novel without the distraction of journalism. He also desired, following the sudden death of his first wife Eileen, to raise their adopted son in a region remote enough to escape the worst of a feared nuclear war. "The only hope," he wrote, "is to have a home with a few animals in some place not worth a bomb."

He arrived on Jura for his last stay on July 28, 1948, traveling from Hairmyres Hospital in East Kilbride, near Glasgow, where he had spent seven months being treated for tuberculosis. Now, returning to the island and still weak, he was determined to finish *1984* before it finished him.

Hairmyres is a short drive from my house, and so on July 28, 2017, I set out to follow in the footsteps of Orwell's final journey.

The hospital has been rebuilt since his day. The only old part left is the ward where it is thought he was treated. A two-story pavilion, it sits on a hill with long views south. No photographs of Orwell exist from his time at Hairmyres, but in the hospital library, in an unordered file of old black-and-whites, I found an intriguing print. It shows the ward as it would have appeared in the forties, on a steep slope overlooking fields. A patient is sitting out on the veranda, no doubt taking the high clean air into his labored lungs. This man is too far away to identify, but there is something about his height and profile. Would it be going too far to imagine a curiously crucified expression on that face?

Orwell's medical treatment was unpleasant. In order that it could be rested, his left lung was collapsed by paralyzing the diaphragm and then pumping air into the abdomen through a needle. He was also given streptomycin, an experimental drug unavailable in Britain, which his friend David Astor, the wealthy editor of the *Observer*, arranged to be imported from the United States. Unfortunately, he developed a severe allergic reaction. His nails and hair began to fall out. He had ulcers in his mouth and throat, blisters on his lips. "At night," he wrote in his diary, "these burst & bled considerably, so that in the morning my lips were always stuck together with blood & I had to bathe them before I could open my mouth."

As best he could, he continued to make progress on *1984*. The doctors grew used to the strong smell of his hand-rolled cigarettes, and to the sound of his typing in bed. It was the latter that seemed to concern them. His right arm was put in a cast for three months, said to have been done to stop him writing. However, Bruce Dick, the grandson and namesake of the eminent tuberculosis specialist who treated Orwell, told me a family legend which suggests that the author found an unexpected collaborator in his attempts to keep working against medical advice. Dick recalled, "The story my gran used to tell was that she would buy paper for him to type on, and take it to him in the hospital." It is a delicious thought: the doctor who kept him alive long enough to complete the book; the doctor's wife who made sure he did not waste the time he was given.

Orwell had made arrangements for the manuscript of *1984* to be destroyed if unfinished at the time of his death. However, by the summer of 1948 he was well enough to return to Jura. The journey from Glasgow, in those days, took at least seven hours: a train, a bus, two boats, and—at the end of all that—an eight mile walk across the island to Barnhill, the house he had leased.

It is still not an easy thing to get to Jura, but I did it as simply as possible, driving a hundred miles or so to the village of Craobh Haven on the Craignish peninsula, and then hiring a local skipper to make the forty-five minute crossing in his launch, *Farsain*. The name is Gaelic for "wanderer," which seemed right for a boat taking us to Orwell's final home; after all his wanderings—Spain, Burma, the London flophouses and Paris slums—this is where he wished to settle.

We headed southwest, straight into the wind. Waves banged the hull. Jura was a dark hump under a grey mantle. A line of three guillemots, flying ellipses, skimmed the water as we put into Kinuachdrachd Bay.

Barnhill is more or less unchanged since Orwell's day. A large white farmhouse overlooking the Sound of Jura, it is owned by the same family, the Fletchers, who had rented it to Orwell. Although available as a vacation rental, it remains a private home, a fact which has not deterred Orwell pilgrims, whose devotion carries their feet along the five-mile track from Ardlussa, where the road runs out.

"My parents have come downstairs to find people have made themselves at home in the kitchen, which doesn't always go down well," said Rob Fletcher, who was staying for a while with his wife and children and had agreed to show me around.

Rob is thirty-seven, so he never met Orwell, but his grandparents, Margaret and Robin, knew him. Margaret later recalled their first encounter: "He arrived at the front door looking very thin and gaunt and worn. I was immediately struck by the very sad face he had. . . . He looked as if he'd been through a great deal."

Orwell lived at Barnhill with his son Richard and sister Avril. They were joined by Bill Dunn, a former army officer who had come to Jura to farm, and who later married Avril. The author remains present in the house in the form of photographs. That wry-looking picture from the front of his press card is framed on the mantelpiece in the living room, arranged among other objects as a near–still life: an antler, a round green bottle, a small brass candlestick with a waterfall of wax cascading over the rim. It wants only a skull, perhaps that one Orwell found on the beach, to make this vanitas complete.

Rob asked if I would like to see Orwell's bedroom, and led the way. It is neither wise nor useful to treat Orwell like a holy martyr, but it was impossible not to pause for a moment at the foot of the staircase, lay one's palm on the finial of the newel post—worn smooth by many hands—and think, "I am touching a place that he touched."

He slept and wrote in a room above the kitchen. It has a low ceiling and a washbowl in one corner. A narrow window looks over the water to mainland Scotland. Rain ran down the glass. A buzzard hovered at the bottom of the garden. "I think he had a desk here in the window," Rob said.

There is nothing in *1984*, its torture chambers and fetid rooms, to suggest this view. In any case, when Orwell returned from Hairmyres, he spent most of his time in bed, sitting up to type, coughing blood. Any kind of physical effort, or simply getting cold, made him feel unwell and his temperature would climb to a suggestive figure—101 degrees. So he kept to his bedroom, the door and windows shut, the air perfumed with paraffin from the stove and smoke from his thick black tobacco. He completed the book in November 1948.

"He came down from his room and said, 'Well, I've finished it,'" Dunn recalled in the book *Remembering Orwell* (published, appropriately enough, in 1984). "And we celebrated by opening the last bottle of wine we had in the place. And Avril said to him, 'What's the title, what are you going to call it?' And he said, 'I think *Nineteen Eighty-Four*.'"

Two months later, he left Jura for a sanatorium, never to return.

Ross

Orwell did not intend *1984* to be his final book. Nevertheless, it is a death-haunted work. It is sometimes said that the novel killed Orwell. Taylor believes so. Can he detect that in the book? I asked. Is it obviously written by a dying man?

"That's interesting," Taylor replied. "There have been several medics with experience of chronic lung disease, especially TB, who have written about the psychopathology of that novel. I've heard it said that there is a kind of hallucinatory quality about some of the book which is characteristic of the tuberculosis sufferer. There is certainly a kind of lurid, end-of-tether quality—some of the terror, Winston Smith and the rats. . . ."

In London, I had asked Richard Blair about his own attitude toward *1984*. Did he resent the novel that had orphaned him? He looked startled. "No, never. I was far too young to be aware of what was happening. I knew he was ill, but I didn't know precisely what it was. I used to ask, when I'd go to see him at the sanatorium, 'Where does it hurt?'"

Blair was on Jura with his aunt Avril and Dunn when he learned, on the radio, that his father had died. This would have been January 21, 1950. "None of us were prepared. It was the eight o' clock news on the Home Service. It just said, 'The death has been announced of George Orwell, author of the dystopian novel *1984*.' I was suddenly confronted with something I didn't understand. Everyone was in a panic."

He was five and a half when his father died. He has had to be careful, growing up, that his own memories do not become a palimpsest overlaid by the recollections of others. Blair had pointed to a poster of Orwell advertising *1984* Live. "I see his face every day. Ever since he died, that face has always been around. So I don't forget."

It must be strange, though. He is your dad, and then he dies, and suddenly he belongs to the world? Blair nodded at this. "Most people don't realize, of course, that his name was Eric Blair. So I can stand right up next to him in public and nobody sees me. That suits me fine. I can be right up at the ringside without people knowing who I am.

"George Orwell belongs to other people, but Eric Blair is mine. I tend to refer to him now as Orwell, almost in the third person."

"And what," I asked Blair, "did you call him?"

"Daddy," he replied.

ON FEBRUARY 3 of this year, Christin Evans, the owner of San Francisco's Booksmith, placed a sign on the counter of her store. "Read up! Fight back!" had been written in red pen next to a drawing of a clenched fist. "A mystery benefactor has bought these copies of *1984* for you if you need one." Stacked behind this notice were fifty copies of Orwell's novel. They had soon all gone, and other customers were donating more. It was, Booksmith explained by email, "a quiet form of resistance."

The original donor is a woman, a linguist, an immigrant to America. She agreed to talk to me on the condition that no more was revealed about her identity. The idea of giving away *1984* came to her about a month after the U.S. election. Trump's victory, and the rise of "alternative facts" as an everyday concept, had left her feeling powerless and afraid: "I'm not allowed to vote, I'm not an American citizen, so I thought, 'OK, how can I make an impact?'"

She had first read *1984* in her early teens, and found it taught her to think critically about society. She reread parts of it in the months leading up to the election, and was struck by how it resonated with her newfound fear of expressing political opinions; perhaps she and her family would be asked to leave the country they had made their home.

There are those who would say that comparisons between Oceania and the United States are fanciful and hyperbolic, that things are not that bad and are not going to get that bad. But *1984*, according to the donor, is a sort of fairy story. It is a frightening tale of gingerbread houses and dark woods intended to scare readers onto the path of resistance. "I think it tells the story of what can happen if you don't do anything," she said. "The moment you give up all your autonomy and agency to the state, you are lost."

In an article for TomDispatch, Rebecca Gordon, a professor of philosophy at the University of San Francisco and expert on torture, summarizes the various pieces of "inconvenient" information—on subjects including climate change and the travel ban—that have been removed from federal websites and Trump's own presidential campaign site since he took office. The present administration, she argues, "seems intent on tossing recent history down the memory hole." This is a reference to the work of Oceania's Ministry of Truth, wherein the events of the past, as reported by newspapers and other media, are constantly altered to remain in line with whatever best suits the state's agenda. The unredacted versions are destroyed—placed in the "memory hole" and burned—and new reports fabricated by expert propagandists. "Who controls the past," Orwell wrote, "controls the future: who controls the present controls the past." It is, perhaps, not so different from lying about the size of a crowd, or where Obama was born, or whether Muslims on a rooftop in New Jersey celebrated as the twin towers fell.

According to the *Washington Post*, Donald Trump made 492 false or misleading claims during his first 100 days in office. Does Gordon really believe that this is a deliberate strategy, that the president is, in her words, "grinding away at American memories" as a means of imposing his narrative and will on the public? "I have to be careful in imputing intentionality to Trump himself," she replied when I called and asked her this. "But the people who are manipulating him, and are competing with each other to manipulate him, very well understand that it is possible through constant repetition of a big lie to create a reality that is different from what I might call consensus reality."

I thought of this while watching the president's speech to supporters at the Phoenix Convention Center on August 22, in the aftermath of Charlottesville. This was his Make American Great Again Rally. He quoted his earlier condemnation of the "egregious display of bigotry, hatred, and violence" that left three dead in the Virginia city, but left out those infamous lines—"on many sides, on many sides"—which seemed to make a moral equivalence between white nationalists and those who had come out to protest them. Just six little words erased from the end of a sentence; it would have been an easy job for even the simplest drone in the Ministry of Truth.

The purpose of this sort of manipulation of reality, in Gordon's view, is not just to make the American public accept official government lines, but to truly believe them. To illustrate this point, she referred to the torture scene in *1984*. Winston is strapped to a machine, some instrument of wrenching torment. His interrogator, O'Brien, holds up four fingers and insists there are five. Every time Winston says otherwise, O'Brien turns a lever that increases the pain surging through his body. This continues until Winston not only agrees there are five fingers, but actually sees them. "In a way," Gordon reflected, "they are turning up the machine on all of us."

IN SENATE HOUSE, *1984* Live was moving toward its end. There was the song of the thrush and the sting of the truncheons. Winston and his lover Julia, imagining themselves safe in their secret room, were about to be arrested by the Thought Police. Meanwhile Winston mused upon Big Brother: "His function is to act as a focusing point for love, fear, and

Ross

reverence, emotions which are more easily felt towards an individual than towards an organization."

I heard those words and wondered, "Is that Trump?" Bonnie Greer thought not. The president is not intelligent enough, in her view. Greer, an American playwright and broadcaster who lives in London, first encountered *1984* on television as a child growing up on Chicago's South Side in the early 1960s. It was a telecast of the 1956 film, starring Edmond O'Brien and Jan Sterling: "Black and white, very bleak, and being a Cold War–baby everything was about the Soviet Union and what they're going to do to you."

These days she sees the story differently. Orwell's novel is "a handbook for now," she told me, and its central message is, "as young black kids are saying, 'Stay woke.' It's about staying awake, staying rebellious, staying human. We're in a power struggle to hold on to fact, to say, 'This is a lie.' If we keep doing that, we can defeat this."

Greer had been given a challenge and an honor; she was to read the final part of the book—from the last, sad encounter with Julia to Winston's final submission. "He had won the victory over himself," she said, speaking softly, even dreamily into the darkness. "He loved Big Brother."

It was curious that such a pessimistic book, such a bleak conclusion, did not seem so in that moment. All day this feeling had been growing. Read *1984* alone in your room and it seems like nothing but sorrow. But here, as a communal experience, it felt like something else: defiance. People had come together to read from a book, or else to simply listen to it, and such a thing will not change the world, or a regime, but as an assertion of a certain kind of civilization it is powerful enough.

Curious, too, that the book's appendix had not been read. This decision was made to save time and for reasons of drama. "The Principles of Newspeak," with which *1984* concludes, is academic, rather dry.

Some have detected in it a note of optimism that is not present in the narrative, but it would certainly have been a flat ending to the day if the event had finished on several pages outlining the form and purpose of Oceania's official language.

Still, it might have been apt.

The ruling regime of Oceania developed Newspeak to make it impossible to articulate—or even conceive of—ideas that went against the ideology of the state. This would mean that older texts could not be translated if they did not conform to Party orthodoxy. Take the Declaration of Independence, for example: "We hold these truths to be self-evident, that all men are created equal"; that if government goes against the unalienable rights of the people, then the people can change the government. Such ideas cannot be rendered in Newspeak; there is simply no equivalent vocabulary. The only possibility, Orwell wrote, is to replace Thomas Jefferson's words with a single expression: *crimethink*.

We live in days when violence of this sort is being done, by the highest in the land, to our language—Sad! Bad! Fake!—and to the very idea of America. Trump is a reductive force: he wants everything to be as small and mean as his own heart, and he has made a start with words. Orwell's *1984*, dark as it is, prefers to regard the human spirit —its capacity to love—as rather a large thing that can endure much. This is perhaps why the book is finding a place in so many American homes. Yes, it is a warning, just as it was in 1949, but it also offers an example and a glint of light.

If there is hope, it lies in the prose.

Ross

Philip K. Dick and the Fake Humans

Henry Farrell

THIS IS NOT the dystopia we were promised. We are not learning to love Big Brother, who lives, if he lives at all, on a cluster of server farms, cooled by environmentally friendly technologies. Nor have we been lulled by Soma and subliminal brain programming into a hazy acquiescence to pervasive social hierarchies.

Dystopias tend toward fantasies of absolute control, in which the system sees all, knows all, and controls all. And our world is indeed one of ubiquitous surveillance. Phones and household devices produce trails of data, like particles in a cloud chamber, indicating our wants and behaviors to companies such as Facebook, Amazon, and Google. Yet the information thus produced is imperfect and classified by machine-learning algorithms that themselves make mistakes. The efforts of these businesses to manipulate our wants leads to further complexity. It is becoming ever harder for companies to distinguish the behavior which they want to analyze from their own and others' manipulations.

This does not look like totalitarianism unless you squint very hard indeed. As the sociologist Kieran Healy has suggested, sweeping political critiques of new technology often bear a strong family resemblance to the arguments of Silicon Valley boosters. Both assume that the technology works as advertised, which is not necessarily true at all.

Standard utopias and standard dystopias are each perfect after their own particular fashion. We live somewhere queasier—a world in which technology is developing in ways that make it increasingly hard to distinguish human beings from artificial things. The world that the Internet and social media have created is less a system than an ecology, a proliferation of unexpected niches, and entities created and adapted to exploit them in deceptive ways. Vast commercial architectures are being colonized by quasi-autonomous parasites. Scammers have built algorithms to write fake books from scratch to sell on Amazon, compiling and modifying text from other books and online sources such as Wikipedia, to fool buyers or to take advantage of loopholes in Amazon's compensation structure. Much of the world's financial system is made out of bots—automated systems designed to continually probe markets for fleeting arbitrage opportunities. Less sophisticated programs plague online commerce systems such as eBay and Amazon, occasionally with extraordinary consequences, as when two warring bots bid the price of a biology book up to $23,698,655.93 (plus $3.99 shipping).

In other words, we live in Philip K. Dick's future, not George Orwell's or Aldous Huxley's. Dick was no better a prophet of technology than any science fiction writer, and was arguably worse than most. His imagined worlds jam together odd bits of fifties' and sixties' California with rocket ships, drugs, and social speculation. Dick usually wrote in a hurry and for money, and sometimes under the influence of drugs or a recent and urgent personal religious revelation.

Still, what he captured with genius was the ontological unease of a world in which the human and the abhuman, the real and the fake, blur together. As Dick described his work (in the opening essay to his 1985 collection, *I Hope I Shall Arrive Soon*):

> The two basic topics which fascinate me are "What is reality?" and "What constitutes the authentic human being?" Over the twenty-seven years in which I have published novels and stories I have investigated these two interrelated topics over and over again.

These obsessions had some of their roots in Dick's complex and ever-evolving personal mythology (in which it was perfectly plausible that the "real" world was a fake, and that we were all living in Palestine sometime in the first century AD). Yet they were also based on a keen interest in the processes through which reality is socially constructed. Dick believed that we all live in a world where "spurious realities are manufactured by the media, by governments, by big corporations, by religious groups, political groups—and the electronic hardware exists by which to deliver these pseudo-worlds right into heads of the reader." He argued:

> the bombardment of pseudo-realities begins to produce inauthentic humans very quickly, spurious humans—as fake as the data pressing at them from all sides. My two topics are really one topic; they unite at this point. Fake realities will create fake humans. Or, fake humans will generate fake realities and then sell them to other humans, turning them, eventually, into forgeries of themselves. So we wind up with fake humans inventing fake realities and then peddling them to other fake humans.

In Dick's books, the real and the unreal infect each other, so that it becomes increasingly impossible to tell the difference between them. The worlds of the dead and the living merge in *Ubik* (1969), the experiences of a disturbed child infect the world around him in *Martian Time-Slip* (1964), and consensual drug-based hallucinations become the vector for an invasive alien intelligence in *The Three Stigmata of Palmer Eldritch* (1965). Humans are impersonated by malign androids in *Do Androids Dream of Electric Sheep?* (1968) and "Second Variety" (1953); by aliens in "The Hanging Stranger" (1953) and "The Father-Thing" (1954); and by mutants in "The Golden Man" (1954).

This concern with unreal worlds and unreal people led to a consequent worry about an increasing difficulty of distinguishing between them. Factories pump out fake Americana in *The Man in the High Castle* (1962), mirroring the problem of living in a world that is not, in fact, the real one. Entrepreneurs build increasingly human-like androids in *Do Androids Dream of Electric Sheep?*, reasoning that if they do not, then their competitors will. Figuring out what is real and what is not is not easy. Scientific tools such as the famous Voight-Kampff test in *Do Androids Dream of Electric Sheep?* (and *Blade Runner*, Ridley Scott's 1982 movie based loosely on it) do not work very well, leaving us with little more than hope in some mystical force—the *I Ching*, God in a spray can, a Martian water-witch—to guide us back toward the real.

We live in Dick's world—but with little hope of divine intervention or invasion. The world where we communicate and interact at a distance is increasingly filled with algorithms that appear human, but are not—fake people generated by fake realities. When Ashley Madison, a dating site for people who want to cheat on their spouses, was hacked, it turned out that tens of thousands of the women on the site were fake "fembots" programmed to send millions of chatty messages to male customers, so as to delude them into thinking that they were surrounded by vast numbers of potential sexual partners.

These problems are only likely to get worse as the physical world and the world of information become increasingly interpenetrated in an Internet of (badly functioning) Things. Many of the aspects of Joe Chip's future world in *Ubik* look horrendously dated to modern eyes: the archaic role of women, the assumption that nearly everyone smokes. Yet the door to Joe's apartment—which argues with him and refuses to open because he has not paid it the obligatory tip—sounds ominously plausible. Someone, somewhere, is pitching this as a viable business plan to Y Combinator or the venture capitalists in Menlo Park.

This invasion of the real by the unreal has had consequences for politics. The hallucinatory realities in Dick's worlds—the empathetic religion of *Do Androids Dream of Electric Sheep?*, the drug-produced worlds of *The Three Stigmata of Palmer Eldritch*, the quasi–Tibetan Buddhist death realm of *Ubik*—are usually experienced by many people, like the television shows of Dick's America. But as network television has given way to the Internet, it has become easy for people to create their own idiosyncratic mix of sources. The imposed media consensus that Dick detested has shattered into a myriad of different realities, each with its own partially shared assumptions and facts. Sometimes this creates tragedy or near-tragedy. The deluded gunman who stormed into Washington, D.C.'s Comet Ping Pong pizzeria had been convinced by online conspiracy sites that it was the coordinating center for Hillary Clinton's child–sex trafficking ring.

Such fractured worlds are more vulnerable to invasion by the non-human. Many Twitter accounts are bots, often with the names and stolen photographs of implausibly beautiful young women, looking to pitch this or that product (one recent academic study found that between 9 and 15 percent of all Twitter accounts are likely fake). Twitterbots vary in sophistication from automated accounts that do no more than retweet what other bots have said, to sophisticated algorithms deploying so-called "Sybil attacks," creating fake identities in peer-to-peer networks to invade specific organizations or degrade particular kinds of conversation.

Twitter has failed to become a true mass medium, but remains extraordinarily important to politics, since it is where many politicians, journalists, and other elites turn to get their news. One research project suggests that around 20 percent of the measurable political discussion around the last presidential election came from bots. Humans appear to be no better at detecting bots than we are, in Dick's novel, at detecting replicant androids: people are about as likely to retweet a bot's message as the message of another human being. Most notoriously, the current U.S. president recently retweeted a flattering message that appears to have come from a bot densely connected to a network of other bots, which some believe to be controlled by the Russian government and used for propaganda purposes.

In his novels Dick was interested in seeing how people react when their reality starts to break down. A world in which the real commingles with the fake, so that no one can tell where the one ends and the other begins, is ripe for paranoia. The most toxic consequence of social media manipulation, whether by the Russian government or others, may have nothing to do with its success as propaganda. Instead, it is that it sows an existential distrust. People simply do not know what or who to believe anymore. Rumors that are spread by Twitterbots merge into other rumors about the ubiquity of Twitterbots, and whether this or that trend is being driven by malign algorithms rather than real human beings.

Such widespread falsehood is especially explosive when combined with our fragmented politics. Liberals' favorite term for the right-wing propaganda machine, "fake news," has been turned back on them by conservatives, who treat conventional news as propaganda, and hence ignore it. On the obverse, it may be easier for many people on the liberal left to blame Russian propaganda for the last presidential election than to accept that many voters had a very different understanding of America than they do.

Farrell

Dick had other obsessions—most notably the politics of Richard Nixon and the Cold War. It is not hard to imagine him writing a novel combining an immature and predatory tycoon (half Arnie Kott, half Jory Miller) who becomes the president of the United States, secret Russian political manipulation, an invasion of empathy-free robotic intelligences masquerading as human beings, and a breakdown in our shared understanding of what is real and what is fake.

These different elements probably would not cohere particularly well, but as in Dick's best novels, the whole might still work, somehow. Indeed, it is in the incongruities of Dick's novels that salvation is to be found (even at his battiest, he retains a sense of humor). Obviously, it is less easy to see the joke when one is living through it. Dystopias may sometimes be grimly funny—but rarely from the inside.

A Strategy for Ruination

China Miéville interviewed by Boston Review

Writing about China Miéville in the *Guardian*, fantasy luminary Ursula K. Le Guin opined, "You can't talk about Miéville without using the word 'brilliant.'" Miéville is a rare sort of polyglot, an acclaimed novelist—he has won nearly every award for fantasy and science fiction that there is, often multiple times—who is equally comfortable in the worlds of politics and academia. Combining his skills as a storyteller and Marxist theorist, his most recent book, *October*, regales readers with the key events of the Russian Revolution. In this interview, Miéville discusses the intersections between his creative oeuvre and the political projects of utopia and dystopia.

BOSTON REVIEW: You are often quoted as saying that you want to write a book in every genre. Nonetheless, many of your books have centered around themes of utopia and dystopia. Do you feel as though dystopia has finally, well-and-truly slipped the bounds of genre?

CHINA MIÉVILLE: Dystopia and utopia are themes, optics, viruses that can infect any field or genre. Hence you find utopian, dystopian, and heterotopian aspects in stories across the board: westerns, romances, crime—let alone, more obviously, in science fiction, speculative fiction, and fantasy.

To the extent that, *before anything else*, texts are -topias (particularly utopias) narrowly conceived—warnings, suggestions, cookbooks, or proposals—they are mostly uninteresting to me. Still, the often-repeated slur that utopias are "dull" has never been politically innocent: it bespeaks reaction. When Emil Cioran attacks utopias for lacking the "rupture" of real life—"the totality of sleeping monsters"—he ignores the ruptures and monsters that lurk in -topias too. As texts, -topias get interesting to the extent that they deviate, underperform, or do too much. Rather the excess of the Big Rock Candy Mountain, with its cigarette trees and lemonade springs, than the plod of Edward Bellamy's *Looking Backward* (1888). In their conflicts, aporias, and surpluses, they can captivate. Alexander Bogdanov's 1908 science fiction novel *Red Star*, for example, is fairly stodgy gruel until the protagonist, Leonid, veers unexpectedly and seemingly off-script through madness and the pedagogy gets opaque.

None of which is to argue against -topias of any prefix, still less of utopian yearning tout court. They are indispensable. But the -topian drive is more contradictory and succulent than some of its vulgar advocates, no less than its critics, make out.

BR: Do you find, in this moment of political nadir, that your sense of the kinds of utopias or dystopias that you want to talk about has changed? This may be another way of asking, as you do in "The Limits of Utopia," whether there are better ways to despair or worse ways to hope right now.

CM: It is hard to avoid the sense that these are particularly terrible days, that dystopia is bleeding vividly into the quotidian, and hence, presumably, into "realism," if that was ever a category in which one was interested. At this point, however, comes an obligatory warning about the historical ubiquity of the questionable belief that Things Have Got Worse, and of the sheer arrogance of despair, the aggrandisement of thinking that one lives in the Worst Times.

But hot on the heels of *that*, we need a countercorrective to a no-less arrogant assumption that things will likely be alright, out of fear that thinking otherwise would indeed be arrogant. Against surrender to the complacency and historical myopia of steady-state politics—of precluding, as a real possibility, epochal degeneration.

There has not in living memory been a better time to be a fascist. I think these are dreadful, sadistic times, getting worse—though with abrupt and salutary countertendencies—and there is no reason that their end point might not be utter catastrophe. For me, facing that is urgent, as is the deployment (or anti-moralist rehabilitation) of categories such as "decadence" and "Barbarism" (as in "Socialism or . . .").

It is not as if the world has not long, long been one in which vast numbers live in dystopian depredation. The horizon is more visible now to many who had thought themselves insulated, if they thought about it at all. And dystopia for some is utopia for others. To repeat something I have said elsewhere, we live in a utopia: it just isn't ours.

Certainly there are better and worse ways to hope and to despair. Despair need not—should not—mean surrender, as anyone who has read John Berger on Palestinians' "stance of undefeated despair" knows. And hope, as Terry Eagleton insists, is not optimism. The former is necessary *and* (because the two are not coterminous) indicated; the latter is a hectoring vacuity, at least as often a fetter as a force for progress.

Miéville

That is not to say optimism is never legitimate—I am considerably more optimistic since the Jeremy Corbyn Event, the unexpected consolidation of power by a principled socialist at the head of the British Labour Party, than I was scant weeks previously—but it has to be specific to the concrete. Optimism, like pessimism and hope, has to be earned.

BR: The terms "salvage" and "salvagepunk" are often associated with your work. In *Railsea* (2012), you portray a world in which denizens of the future survive by grazing on the trash of our civilization, finding in those remnants the components they need to make a life. You have also collaborated on launching a magazine, *Salvage*. What role do you think salvage and bricolage must play in imagining a viable future?

CM: Salvage keeps me going. And obviously not only me: clearly also, for example, my collaborator (and coiner of the term "salvagepunk") Evan Calder Williams, and my comrades at the journal *Salvage*, particularly Rosie Warren, Richard Seymour, and Jamie Allinson.

Why is not quite clear: there is always something evasive about why particular metaphors resonate as they do. Which is fine by me. Of the various concepts that are politically/aesthetically powerful and formative—helpful—to me, salvage has for a long time been *primus inter pares*. Word-magic. A retconned syncretic backformation from "salvation" and "garbage." A homage to, rather than repudiation of, the trash-world wanderers and breakfasters-among-the-ruins that always transfixed me. An undefeated despair: "despair" because *it's done*, this *is* a dystopia, a worsening one, and dreams of interceding *just in time* don't just miss the point but are actively unhelpful; "undefeated" because it is worth fighting even for ashes, because there are better and much, much worse ways of being too late. Because *and yet*.

This shit is where we are. A junk heap of history and hope. I am done with the Procrustean strategy of whipping playbooks out of our pockets and squinting to make what we see fit their schema. These days—these particular astounding days—I can't politically take seriously anyone who still refuses to be surprised, anyone faithful to the cosplay radicalism of the know-it-all left, of permanent preemptive certainty. But bricolage precisely because this is not about some arrogant sneer of revisionism, of "new times"–posturing dispensing with tradition: it's about scrabbling to put its scobs together anew. It's too late to *save*, but we might repurpose. Suturing, jerry-rigging, cobbling together. Finding unexpected resources in the muck, using them in new ways. A strategy for ruination. For all of us at *Salvage*, this is a redoubled radical commitment, a groping for emancipation. (Please subscribe!)

BR: This seems related to an avatar that you propose for our age: the "porcupine angel," a creature who takes shelter from the winds of history within the wreck of civilization itself.

CM: I mooted the "porcupine angel," *Angelus erethizon*, as an exemplary figure chimera-ed from two travelers in the storm of history: Walter Benjamin's back-blown angel, and Ursula K. Le Guin's articulation of a Swampy Cree notion of the porcupine bracing itself in a crevice in the face of danger, "to speculate safely on an inhabitable future." We are buffeted, but still we might brace, and bristle.

What is most vivid for me in the porcupine angel is its motion. It is too squat and heavy to fly. It stilt-walks, instead, on its wingtips. A motion that seems for a moment quite new, but that we realize we have seen before. When we watch bats crawl. Faced with unusual difficulties, certain animals move in deeply strange, unfamiliar ways, ways that seem abruptly alien, and/but that remain absolutely *theirs*.

Miéville

Occult motion, part of, hidden in, their quiddities. Watch those bats pick their wingtip ways. Watch octopuses stilt-walk on weirdly stiff limbs, watch hares or horses swim. In those moments utopia feels so close it is hard to breathe.

BR: Your new book, *October*, is a novelistic retelling of the Russian Revolution. You begin it with a quote from Alexander Kaun: "One need not be a prophet to foretell that the present order of things will have to disappear." If Marx is right that history repeats itself, "first as tragedy, then as farce," does it feel to you as though, on the hundredth anniversary of the Russian Revolution, Donald Trump's rise to power on a populist tide represents a farcical betrayal of the spirit of revolution?

CM: We have to be careful about our terms. I've no particular beef with "populist" as a shorthand or placeholder, but the problem—especially when it comes before the word "tide"—is that it can imply there is something fundamental shared across all broadly anti- or non-centrist political projects. That is what lies behind the plethora of—maliciously or criminally stupid—headlines conjoining Trump, Corbyn, Bernie Sanders, and even Marine Le Pen.

Trump came to power due to a number of factors: a radicalized Republican base drawn by his consolidation of various racist ideologemes, for the propagation of which Democrat leadership, as well as Republican, bears deep responsibility; clusters of previous Obama voters in the Rust Belt flipping in the face of a wretched, contemptuous campaign by an entitled neoliberal hawk; a deeply undemocratic system; and, in places, collapsing voter turnout, thanks to a systemic hollowing-out of democracy that centrists have long been perfectly happy to accommodate. Such specifics tell us a lot more about how we got to this catastrophic situation, and what we might do to get out of it, than a more nebulous anxiety about "populism."

It is perfectly, abundantly true that the technocratic, centrist, socially neoliberal project of the Democrats and New Labour (to name but two) is in major crisis, and that in the cracks new forms grow. I mourn that project not one iota. It deserves to die, and the jeremiads about its passing are overwhelmingly predicated on elitism and nostalgia. What does not follow, of course—see Trump—is that whatever rises in the rubble is an improvement.

Certainly, for me, a radical, systemic change is the best hope we have for moving away from this system of sadism, and I hold the alt-center's hope for a return to the status quo ante (rule by "the adults in the room") to be not only an indefensible project but a doomed one. So yes, a wholly different kind of project—a revolutionary one, an upheaval, an overturning of existing social priorities and dynamics—is what we deserve, and the unhesitant demand for it is by far our best hope.

BR: Is it part of your project in *October* to reach general readers to inform them, first, of what real political revolution looks like and, second, that it is not a foregone conclusion that revolution ends badly?

CM: I would express the "aims" of my "project" (vis-à-vis writing) cautiously, not because they are not real but because the mediations between intent, text, and reader are so very many and various. With *October*, I hope, first, that those who wanted to know more about the world-historic moment of the Russian Revolution will be somewhat swept up in the revolution's rhythms, and come away with a clearer sense of, literally, what happened, when, to whom, and of course why. What those who fought were fighting for. And I hope to make a case that whatever one's opinion of the politics, or of the revolutionary project's chances, that the liberal or right-wing nostrum that this utopian yearning was always doomed is not just unjustified, it's an abdication of analysis. An effort to pick apart what ultimately went so terribly wrong is a universe away from the dutiful, rote assertion that it was always going to go wrong. The revolution remains an intense inspiration to me.

br: Did writing *October* change (or reinforce) your views about the uses and limits of political violence?

cm: My attitude toward political violence was not particularly altered by the research. I did come away with a reinforced certainty that, however tempting it is to turn necessities into virtues, it is a dreadful mistake. By any means necessary, of course. Which does not mean the celebration of any necessary means, still less the deflation of what counts as "necessary," still less "by any means."

br: In "The Limits of Utopia," you propose the following route toward progress: "A start for any habitable utopia must be to overturn the ideological bullshit of empire and . . . revisit the traduced and defamed cultures on the bones of which some conqueror's utopian dreams were piled up." There is a way in which turning to the past can be a deeply conservative impulse: for example, contemporary evangelicals and biblical literalists contend that they are doing the same, as do many other moralizers, celebrators of the "traditional" family, white supremacists, and men's rights activists. What guidelines can we use when turning to the past to guarantee that our efforts remain progressive? How do we "overturn the ideological bullshit of empire" without becoming the next empire?

CM: I realize this is a discussion that could easily and fruitfully extend to books'-length, so this can only be a ludicrously partial and maybe glib placeholder. But I suspect one way to negotiate this might be to reiterate (repeatedly) that neither memory nor prediction, neither mourning nor anticipation, generate radical, emancipatory politics on their own, any more than they do reactionary, sadistic politics. The question has to be what (like metaphor) they provoke in us in particular circumstance, and, more, how they are deployed. The valence of no memory is a given. I see no reason one can't look both back and forward (and sideways, and diagonally, and inward) to find inspirations.

I honestly don't know why "overturning the ideological bullshit of empire" should necessary make us particularly prone to "becoming the next empire," unless the implication is that "revolutions always eat their children," which is a kind of reactionary tragedianism that I don't accept. That things *might* go wrong, sure, but that would always be about specifics, not simply because we would be in a position of having overturned shit. Whatever difficulties would follow—and they would—that would surely be a good problem to have.

BR: Your novels often deal with themes of radical otherness: human protagonists partner with ancient gods and personified oceans (as in 2010's *Kraken*), and, in *Embassytown* (2011), with the alien Hosts, whose prelapsarian language makes them incapable, without intercession, of communicating with humans or even recognizing us as sentient. Do you feel as though the process of puzzling through such fictional relationships has given you any useful insights into how to bridge more commonplace divides between ourselves and those we consider to be other?

CM: I'd be wary of thinking that any facility in representing alterity would necessarily give a person political insights, about everyday divides or anything else. There are plenty of writers of otherness (including very brilliant ones) whose politics cleave in a very different direction, of course. More fundamentally, I would suggest that any convergence of political and aesthetic thought in that manner is either relatively contingent, or, more to the point, that the line of causality does not run at all neatly from the fiction to the social and political. That is just, I think, not how fiction works, for writer or reader. I don't think, in other words, that it's writing the fiction that has given me political ideas.

The best I can get at the relation is that my head, like all heads, is a saucepan containing a simmering soup of ideas, drives, desiderata, concerns, fascinations, anxieties, insights, opacities. I dole that broth into different bowls using different ladles and set to with different spoons depending on whether I am doing fiction or nonfiction (or anything else). Different dinnerware, same ingredients.

BR: As both a novelist and a political thinker, what kinds of daily practices do you advocate for and gloss when you use "utopia" as a verb, as in "We should utopia as hard as we can"?

CM: Everyone who holds that, first, this shit isn't necessarily it, and, second, that it would be better if it were better, is, to some extent, utopia-ing. (Which of course includes those on the right.) For me, all I can say is that, though I have been extremely politically pessimistic at times, my pessimism has always been founded on an absolute belief not only in the possibility, but the urgent necessity, of fundamental radical change. The political task is to operate with two horizons: that of the immediate aim, the shorter-term, potential gain, the moment-by-moment; and that further, the utter, unsayable. We have talked about this in

Salvage: if you hold, as we do, that—whatever reforms we can and must fight to instantiate—this system can't ultimately be reformed out of being one of exploitation and oppression, then we have to mediate that fight for quotidian amelioration with a strategy of tension, an unflinching antinomianism. To reclaim the slogan from the defeated attempt to oppose Greek austerity measures, an *Oxi* ("no") underlying all. Precisely because it isn't impossible; because of the scale of what it would mean; because of how we'd come to other ourselves in the process, changing ourselves to fit the world we would, will, have remade; far, far more than to outline any particular prescriptions, to utopia must be to say no.

Miéville

Dulltopia

Mark Bould

FREDRIC JAMESON'S ESSAY in *An American Utopia* (2016) begins with the observation, "We have seen a marked diminution in the production of new utopias over the last decades (along with an overwhelming increase in all manner of conceivable dystopias, most of which look monotonously alike)." Jameson recognizes the profligacy with which capitalism, its eye always on the main chance, belches dystopias. At the same time, he regrets its dulling of human creativity and, thus, its homogenization of dystopia. Yearning for richness, he finds formulaic reiteration. Risk-averse publishers gamble millions on the tried-and-tested strategy of more of the (slightly re-jigged) same. As does Hollywood, albeit on greater orders of magnitude.

Nearly 300 pages further into the same book, Slavoj Žižek insists that the "dystopias that abound in recent blockbuster movies and novels (*Elysium*, *The Hunger Games*), although apparently leftist (presenting a postapocalyptic society of extreme class divisions), are unimaginative, monotonous, and also politically wrong."

Where the Marxist locates monotony in the similarity between dystopias, the Lacanian implies that each individual example is tedious, hackneyed, and wrongheaded. I am not entirely convinced by either one.

First, they sound too much like grumpy old men—too much like Adorno, or my dad. Many contemporary dystopias are written for teens, and therefore closer to the iterative, leveling-up video game than the classical narrative structure of Yevgeny Zamyatin, and possessed of an affective politics that may well evade the elder statesmen of leftist critical theory. Their boredom might simply be the kind that Elizabeth Legge calls "an injured sense of one's own centrality." In contrast, I fondly recall my consternated delight at Mark Fisher's enthusiasm for *The Hunger Games: Catching Fire* (2013): "a counter-narrative to capitalist realism," a reveille to wake us from our "hedonic depressive slumber."

Second, because much as I like to imagine our doyens of political and libidinal economy poring over the latest Scott Westerfeld or Ally Condie or James Dashner or Samantha Shannon, I am not persuaded they have done their due diligence. Neither offers any evidence or argumentation. Impression as pronouncement; move right along.

However, others also clearly find repetition overwhelming difference when it comes to contemporary dystopias. Sometimes, as with the film adaptations of Veronica Roth's Divergent series, audiences stay away. Budgets are reassessed. Franchises are cancelled. Intellectual property is "reimagined" for other media.

Or shelved. Destined, after an unconscionably brief hiatus, to be rebooted, leaving us to wonder why Jameson and Žižek seem surprised by the dullness of the dystopia commodity.

Their surprise is surprising in another way, too. Dystopia (the place) is meant to be boring. Every bit as boring as utopia (the place and usually the text). In fact, the anti-utopia, from which dystopia emerged, arose from dissatisfaction with utopia's monodimensional characters and lack of conflict, its stalled narratives and utilitarian designs, its smug certainty and oppressive dullness. By satirically replicating the utopias of Edward Bellamy and H. G. Wells in order to rail against them, anti-utopians insisted upon bourgeois individualism and thus foreclosed possibility. They cast any attempt to imagine or plan social improvement as totalitarianism, as if somehow our world is free and unplanned. As if capitalism and patriarchy and white supremacism were natural. As if somehow—and most incredibly of all—Ayn Rand were right.

Raffaella Baccolini and Tom Moylan locate dystopia on the fractured ground between the historical antinomies of utopia and anti-utopia. It is a contradictory, hybrid form, despairing but not without hope. And, like utopias and anti-utopias, dystopias are strong and stable realms, repressive and unchanging, their inhabitants determined by dominant ideology, or fearfully simulating conformity to it.

Dystopia (the place) only stops being boring when it fails; and that is when dystopia (the text) can become exciting. Often, as in the anti-utopia, failure kicks off with an unanticipated libidinal connection, such as Winston and Julia in *1984* (1949), or Christian Bale and that puppy in *Equilibrium* (2002). Then later there is the running and the screaming. The blowing up of things. The flight into the green space outside the city. And, if the protagonist is really lucky, he has not had a psychotic break. He is not strapped in a torturer's chair. He is not fantasizing escape while humming some old exaltation samba.

BUT LET US SUPPOSE Jameson and Žižek are right. Let us suppose that, one way or another, contemporary dystopias are more monotonous than those of other eras. Why might that be?

One answer might lie in the way SF (science fiction or speculative fiction) functions. Jameson hews closely to the model proposed by Darko Suvin in the seventies: the SF text is dominated by a "novum," a materially plausible novelty or innovation—no magic allowed!—that produces an imaginative world different from the material world the author and reader inhabit (or at least, though he never says it, the world of conventional bourgeois realism). This difference should defamiliarize our own world, producing a sense of "cognitive estrangement" that enables us to see it critically and anew.

But what if forty years of neoliberalism's violently reiterated dogma that "there is no alternative" has left us incapable of imagining not only better worlds but also worse ones? In 2004 political scientist Bruce Tonn discovered that people were "just not able to imagine *any* type of future" more than fifteen to twenty years out. William Gibson suggests that "far more ominous" than the current taste for things dystopian and post-apocalyptic is "how seldom, today, we see the phrase 'the 22nd century.'"

Neoliberalism's "there is no alternative" was always meant to be a self-fulfilling prophecy. It wants the dictatorship of the bourgeoisie to be all there is and all there can be. (By bourgeoisie, I do not mean those poor deluded fools drinking lattes out of avocados, but the capitalist class, itself increasingly a metonym for the algorithms of a global economy that no longer really needs them in order to perpetuate itself.) It wants white supremacist patriarchal capitalist brutality and immiseration. The devastation of the biosphere for profit. The exhaustion of our physical and psychic resources.

We already inhabit the worst of all possible worlds—the one that actually exists—so perhaps there is no critique left that dystopia can effect. Perhaps, reduced to a spectacular commodity, to obscene surface, it has nothing left to tell us that we do not already know. Perhaps its only function now is anti-utopian. To deny, as in The Hunger Games, the possibility of radical change. To urge upon us, as in The Walking Dead, the zero-sum sadocratic ethics of the neoliberal market, where everyone is ultimately—and suddenly, just like that—disposable.

And then, having done this on narrative, thematic, and affective levels, dystopia does it again through its very form as a commodity.

IF DYSTOPIA can no longer gain sufficient distance from our own world to generate the cognitive estrangement upon which SF's political potential hinges, we should not look to the future or to alternate words. We should, for the present, stick with the present. We just need to go deeper. To dive into boredom.

In the February 2010 *Sight & Sound*, Jonathan Romney described a major trend in the new millennium's cinema:

> films that are slow, poetic, contemplative—cinema that downplays event in favour of mood, evocativeness and an intensified sense of temporality. Such films highlight the viewing process itself as a real-time experience in which, ideally, you become acutely aware of every minute, every second spent watching.

With precursors in the structuralist Chantal Akerman, the indifferent Andy Warhol, the deliberate Yasujirō Ozu, the meditative Andrei Tarkovsky, the ambiguous Theo Angelopoulos, the glacial Béla Tarr, slow cinema represents an understandable "thirst for abstraction at a time when immediacy and simultaneity . . . are tyrannical demands." It rewards us with "an exalted reverie."

Two months later, *Sight & Sound* editor Nick James's monthly column complained about these "passive-aggressive" films "demand[ing] great swathes of our precious time to achieve quite fleeting and slender aesthetic and political effects." His discontent reeks of nausea—not some existential *mal de vivre*, but revulsion at the systematic reduction of creative human energies to mere labor-power (including, it perhaps dawned on him, sat there in front of yet another film in which, very slowly, very little happened, his own).

Slow cinema confronts us with the experience of duration, with the boredom that Joseph Brodsky describes as "pure, undiluted time in all its repetitive, redundant, monotonous splendor." The films are often long—Lav Diaz's *Norte, the End of History* (2013) clocks in at 250 minutes, for example, and Wing Bang's *Tie Xi Qu: West of the Tracks* (2002) at 551 minutes. The takes are long, too: while contemporary Hollywood's average shot length is 4 to 6 seconds, dropping as low as 2 (or less) in something like *Resident Evil: Apocalypse* (2007) or *Mad Max: Fury Road* (2015), the average shot length of Mauro Herce's *Dead Slow Ahead* (2015) is 40 seconds, while that of Peter B. Hutton's *At Sea* (2007) is 41.5 seconds.

Cameras are often static; maybe, occasionally, there is an agonizingly slow track or zoom. The lighting and color palette are murkily naturalistic. Or painterly. And, sometimes, stunningly beautiful. Dialogue, when there is dialogue, meanders, peters out. Ambient sound—sometimes terrifyingly immersive—is preferred, but not de rigueur. Characters are opaque, and narratives tenuous. Generically familiar materials are—as in the police procedurals *Police, Adjective* (2009) and *Once Upon a Time in Anatolia* (2011)—distended inconclusively.

Slow cinema cast us adrift, and upon our own resources, in the unstable realms of semiosis and affect.

At Sea: **Part One**

Hutton's hour-long silent film was shot on 16 mm; its muted colors are even more subdued on YouTube, where one is likeliest to watch it. *At Sea* is divided into three parts of roughly equal duration, though the second part contains fewer shots than the others. It depicts the construction of a container ship in South Korea; a container ship's voyage from Montreal to Hamburg; and a maritime graveyard in Bangladesh. Already, by noting where it was filmed, I have given you more information than the film's eighty shots convey.

In the shipyard Hutton's camera hangs back, eager to watch but reluctant to treat humans as its subjects. Working alone, or in twos and threes, the people remain too small for their identities, their actions and interactions, to be discerned. (Is that one really wiping down the bulbous bow by hand? With a cloth?) When, in the distance, a rogue golf umbrella shades workers who are taking a break, you begin to look for other details, other traces of subjectivity. Size defeats you.

Water cascades into the dry dock, insignificant in comparison to the hull from which it spews, but momentous in relation to a truck that drives by, and then insignificant again. A section of crane tower glides horizontally against a blue sky. An elevator cage descends the edge of the screen. Scaffolding, bulkhead girders, gargantuan metal skeletons—there are grids everywhere. A flattened depth of field transforms verticals and diagonals into graphics. A cold constructivism fills the sky with metallic geometries. Suspended from dozens of cables, a component of the ship swings across the screen. But to call it a component gives the impression of something singular and small. It is already a constructed thing, bigger than a house. But here it is just one more piece of a three-dimensional puzzle.

Humans do not belong in an environment of such proportions, among such blocks of matter, such hazardous trajectories. They move things and attach things, they weld and paint, unaware that their only purpose is to provide a sense of scale.

As if to mock those audacious enough to name the completed *Toledo Spirit*, a giant, celebratory red-and-white sphere bursts open alongside it, trailing streamers like an enormous jellyfish, releasing shreds of paper that glitter in the sun as they flock and flutter through the air. More alive, it seems, than the complacent human microorganisms who pose, in suits and uniforms, for the official photo.

No Cronenbergian new flesh, no Ballardian psychosexual accommodation, could possibly fit us to this world. To this actually existing world.

At Sea: Part Two

As the ship eases under a suspension bridge and out to sea, the camera peers through the rain-washed windscreen, over the containers that fill the deck. They are white, green, yellow, red, blue, orange, mustard, the neatly abandoned Tetris of a monstrous toddler. Cloud shadows race over them: light, then shade, then light again. At night, their colors are invisible beneath the ship's lights; their covers ripple.

Sometimes it rains. Sometimes there is sun. When it is cold, ice slides down the windscreen; warmer, and wipers clear away the rain so the camera can properly see the enshrouding fog. A dark smudge to port becomes another ship passing.

The horizon rises and fall, tilts from side to side. The sea runs smoothly. The sea swells. The ship's wake is a curve of gray against a darker gray, beneath a red-brown sky. Looking over the side is like looking at a Mark Rothko painting: a strip of blue sky, a strip of red rail, a strip of the gunwale's shadowed darkness. Then, as the ship tilts, a darker strip of blue—the sea—appears beneath the sky and disappears.

Bould

The sun, haloed in red, bobs up and down amid black clouds, a yellow bouncing ball with no lyrics to follow.

A still dusk. On the horizon a silhouetted ship passes in front of the last curve of a sinking sun.

Clouds and moonlight above are doubled in the sea below, a poorly made Rorschach. Silver-topped waters as black as kraken ink writhe mesmerically. Everything becomes dark.

This is the in-between. The filthy materiality of the financial sublime. There is no Romantic wanderer above this sea of fog, contemplating immensity. Just relentless function, unending subservience. The ship is not built to outlast the world, but to incinerate it. A workhorse of the global market, its own gargantuan carbon emissions unrecorded in any nation's ledger, it accelerates the rate at which oil is burned to make power and plastic to make commodities to make money.

It is inexorable, this end of the world, and much too big to register on 16 mm at 24 frames per second. But there are no people here, only an impassive kino-eye.

Dead Slow Ahead: Weird

Herce's *Dead Slow Ahead* is like a longer, more spectacular rendition of *At Sea*'s second part. Nothing much happens, and what does happens slowly, as the cargo vessel *Fair Lady* weaves an uncertain course from the Black Sea to the Red Sea, then back to the Mediterranean and across the Atlantic. (The film does not tell us this. Indeed, the four shots that are dense with legible information—blueprints, floorplans—race by, relatively speaking, in under a minute and explain nothing.) But Herce's high-resolution digital images, his neo-noir-gone-even-more-sour palette, and his soundtrack of distorted noises and disembodied voices, render an utterly material world in all its sublime weirdness, its stonefaced absurdity.

It begins at night, offshore. Electronics beep. Amid hard-to-decipher bursts of polyglot radio chatter, an automated female voice enunciates in English. There is a machinic throb, an ominous time-golem always just about to arrive. Below, a pitch-black sea undulates; above, the sky, which should be full of stars, is deep reddish brown, filthy with light pollution. In between is a fairytale Manhattan, a skyline of yellow light, garish and unsavory. An unreal city, blazing against the night, a refinery burning down the world. It recalls the end of *White Heat* (1949), the film that takes James Cagney from robbing steam trains to an ultramodern exurban chemical plant, all pipes and silos and vats burgeoning with Armageddon. It also evokes the aerial views of a future Los Angeles in *Blade Runner* (1982) and, lurking behind them, the Port Talbot steelworks on the South Wales coast that inspired Ridley's inferno. But mostly it brings to mind the final shot of *Évolution* (2015), Lucile Hadžihalilović's film about the amphibian mothers of the species that will succeed us once we have brought down the Anthropocene's final curtain.

Equipment clangs and bangs and whirs. Humans in orange overalls, hard helmets, and protective goggles stand by. This dance of indifferent machines and diffident humans has, with all its perilous mass and inertia, been danced a dozen times before, or more. An angular monstrosity, its shape uncertain, rotates, its fell gaze sweeping the scene like the Cenobites' Leviathan in *Hellraiser II* (1988). Steam swirls. Lights flare so bright they obscure more than they reveal. It is a crane, scooping coal (or is it wheat?) from barges and cascading it down into the ship's hold.

Glimpsed through a window, but not heard, the crew desperately karaokes. Later, as if time is a closed, repeating loop, we will be on the other side of the window. The sporadic dance of LED torches provides the only light in their makeshift discotheque. A crewman, smoking, slumps alone by empty beer cans. Off screen, voices wail along tunelessly to Neil Sedaka's "You Mean Everything to Me." The crewman's eyes, Deckard-like, glisten inhuman. The LED flickering becomes insistent. Eyes silver. The karaoke singer belts out an unheard song, overdubbed by the sound of squealing. Like amplified insects, or swine-things from the pit. It goes on much too long.

In daylight, from the deck, a riverbank or shoreline slides by. As in a L. S. Lowry seascape, sky, land, and water are washed out, off-white, and hard to tell apart. Distances are indeterminate. There are no identifiable objects (are those ancient wooden keels rotting in the shallows?) to lend scale.

Then, later, at sea, the ship rolls from side to side, tilting the horizon one way and then the other: a storm cloud ahead, balanced on a column of rain, like a mushroom; a sunset, or a sunrise, just bands of dark and light; a dropping sun eases out from under a dark cloud standing against an abyssal sky. Water above and below. The machinery begins to sound like whale song. Aquatic, amniotic, as if we are being born, and borne, out of this world and into another.

Screens map the ship's motion—to call it progress seems impertinent —through a seeming void. The bleeping of navigational instruments is like a desperate sonar hurled into emptiness.

In the depths of the ship, clean industrial spaces become Gothic, governed by the remorselessly throbbing turbine. Tainted red, it beats. A brutal machine heart, its clanking thumps like an imperialist raconteur's nocturnal native drums. Crewmen, their faces briefly illuminated, peer down pipes and shafts. One scrubs away at a surface. In the impenetrable darkness, hidden edits derange the space; continuous yet impossible, a non-Euclidean geometry. (Later, an unusual high-angle shot down into the engine room Eschers a staircase.)

Soon, though, amid all this dread, there will be comedy.

Dead Slow Ahead: **Absurd**

Three shots, 304 seconds.

On the starboard side of the bridge, the camera looks to port. Through the window opposite, it sees a light blue sky and white clouds. As the ship rolls from side to side, the sea rises into, and then out of, view.

The captain's chair is empty. The bridge is empty. Just bleeps, a creak, a chirring phone.

A crewman enters, but by the time he picks up the receiver whoever is calling has hung up. When it rings again, he picks it up and, his voice registering neither panic nor even concern, reports:

> Attention, please, there's water in the ship. Not only at the bridge's wheels
> but also at the bottom. It's pouring in.
>
> [Pause.]
>
> Yes, more water is entering from the bottom.
>
> [Pause.]
>
> Yes, that's right.
>
> [Pause.]
>
> The water is flowing in!

He hangs up. Ambles out of the frame. The bridge is empty once more. The ship rocks from side to side, creaking. Nothing happens. An electronic squawk. Over the intercom, another voice lacking urgency: "Hello? Sir, here at the Sub-1 there's water, too!"

No response. Squawks. The next voice sounds metallic: "Is anybody listening? An entire river is running through the keel. There's a lot."

Another unhurried voice: "The water is reaching the storage tanks."

Bould

Cut to the view from the captain's chair. Spray from the steel-gray sea washes over the deck and hatches. Beneath the pale sky, clouds fill the horizon, which tilts slowly from side to side. A voice: "Roger! Roger! Attention! The wheat is getting wet."

A phone rings. Someone says: "The wheat."

Cut to black. A phone quavers. Bleeps persist. A final unhurried voice: "Sir, this is a disaster!"

The roaring of the engines merges with the soundtrack.

The pace is wrong. This is not what we expect from a nautical catastrophe. There are no Somalian pirates for Tom Hanks to outfox, no fiery explosions for Mark Wahlberg to outrun. Instead, just a temporal mismatch between humans and physics, the deadpan unfurling of events.

A half hour into the film and this is the first dialogue: voices isolated in different parts of the ship calling out blindly to each other, missing each other. It will be another half hour before dialogue is attempted again.

In the hold, wavelets of red-brown water. On the dunes of wheat, there are long-handled shovels and squat buckets. Not enough men, inadequately equipped, load buckets that once full are winched away. The men sit and wait. The open hatch far above them looks like an ebony monolith into which they might fall. But there is no transcendence here. Just a cursed Earth lapping against the ribs of an unscalable wall.

Topside, the grain is piled on the deck to be blown away or swept away or, eventually, shoveled overboard.

This is not a salvage effort. (In reality, it took the entire crew a month of seventeen-hour days to dump the spoiled cargo into the sea.) The ship ploughs on.

When the floodwater is all that is left, a crewman sits there alone, as if forgotten. This is not why, eons ago, fish crept onto the land.

You have to laugh.

Dead Slow Ahead: **Disconnected**

Once more the ship heads down river, the immobile camera gazing to port, land and sky yet again indistinct, alien. There is another industrial plant in the distance, an enormous tower looming over it like a gargantuan moisture vaporator on a sodden Tatooine.

We pass out to sea in a single five-and-a-half-minute shot. There is no one. The whole world is deserted now, raptured, including the ship. The corridors are empty. In the crew lounge, a muted television plays. A table is set for half a dozen to eat together. A still life of an apple, a plate, a napkin, an upturned glass. Photos of the officers and crew. A whiteboard reminder of upcoming alcohol tests. A solitary voice says, "Hello?" and moments later says it again.

Finally, an automated voice responds: "Sorry, we cannot connect you. Thank you for calling."

This is the final act: brightly lit recesses, pristine pipes and flues. Slow zooms, tilts, and pans that could be a rostrum camera moving over stills were it not for the crewman who jogs through a couple of shots. (He goes past twice, in too-rapid succession, as if his route is badly designed or time is passing differently for him.) And on the soundtrack, crewmen call their families, heartbreakingly mundane conversations thwarted by distance, inadequate technology, insufficient credit.

Elsewhere it is the New Year, but *Fair Lady* is far from land. There is no cell signal. A wife's texts loiter in cyberspace, abstracted from context. On the satellite phone, a man asks, "Are you still beautiful?" as might an interstellar voyager haunted by time dilation.

"Ugly," she replies, worn out.

He tells her he looks at the photo of her and their daughters. Their exchanges of love admit to their resignation over separation. Talking is too difficult. He promises to text.

"We are on course now," he explains to his son. "We're in the middle of the ocean. We still don't know where we are headed. We are just going and going."

He cannot hear his son clearly.

A crewman phones his pregnant wife. He calls the unborn baby Eunice, but she has no idea who he is talking about. Perhaps she has forgotten their earlier conversation about baby names, or maybe he only imagined it.

She wonders who will take her to the hospital when she goes into labor. He should be home by October. If she can hold on until the last week of the month . . . "Your credit has been used up." The line is cut.

A crewman is worried about his sons. There seem to be no problems with them, but the connection is dodgy. He cannot be sure.

The timelag, the intermittent signal, the pauses between sentences make speakers overlap, uncertain that they have been heard. Faltering conversations become incoherent, trail off. Connections are lost.

They might just as well be unsuspecting clones mining Helium-3 on the far side of the Moon. At least then they would have illusions.

The industrial and the material persist, sustaining the electronic-immaterial.

There is a turbine at the heart of it all. It is relentless, imperturbable. Down there in the dark spaces, it churns and does not care.

At Sea: Part Three

In the most harrowing of dystopias, there are always utopian traces.

At Sea ends on a beach. A man sits on a chair beneath an umbrella. Murky water flows by rather than breaking on this shore. Black birds bob around; a small dog plays in the oil-saturated mud. And against the skyline, jagged slabs: whole ships run aground, their hulls to be stripped by men without machines, with just the most basic of tools. There is no safety equipment. Debris falls from overhead. A sledgehammer is wielded against a barnacled rusting hulk. Black smoke pours from a partially dismantled hull. Even on YouTube, you can taste the carcinogens, the slow violence of an elsewhere-commerce shortening lives.

These people of color work together in the detritus of the pallid culture that brought apocalypse. They are not a cargo cult, nor dapper hipster bricoleurs. They salvage, they survive, they persist. They foreshadow the disaster communism that might yet save some of us.

They take a break to kick a ball around in the no man's land of this undeclared war.

In long shot, they do not diminish; we recede.

Gradually, they become aware of the camera. They pose, move closer, stream past it onto unseen ground. Several faces pop back into the frame, really close, to peer into this alien device. But they too move on. We are nothing more than a lens now, an absence. We are gone.

It is customary in moments such as this to evoke Walter Benjamin's Angel of History, who is blown backward by a storm into a future he cannot see, while catastrophe "keeps piling wreckage upon wreckage" at his feet. But that is the wrong angel to end with. The one we need is to be found in Albrecht Dürer's engraving *Melencolia I* (1514). She sits slumped, elbow on knee and head on hand, radiating boredom. Surrounded by the tools of an architect and geometer, she is sick to death of her terrestrial labors and longs to return to the heavens. But there is no surcease. Even her odd-looking dog seems queasy.

Then take a look at her eyes.

She is beyond pissed off. She is fucking furious. (As we should be.)

And she looks ready to tear this shit down. (As we should.)

She is, after all, an architect, and can build something better. (As can we.)

Charlie Jane Anders is the author of *All the Birds in the Sky*, which won the Nebula, Locus, and Crawford Awards, and was on *Time*'s list of the ten best novels of 2016.

Margaret Atwood is the celebrated author of more than twenty works of fiction. In 2017 her award-winning novel, *The Handmaid's Tale*, was turned into a television series that won five Emmys.

Adrienne Bernhard is a writer and editor who lives in New York City.

Mark Bould teaches film and literature at the University of the West of England. He coedits the journal *Science Fiction Film and Television* and the book series Studies in Global Science Fiction.

Thea Costantino is an Australian artist based in the UK. She is Head of Visual Arts in the School of Creative Arts at the University of Hertfordshire.

Junot Díaz is author of the highly-acclaimed short story collections *Drown* and *This Is How You Lose Her* as well as the Pulitzer Prize–winning novel *The Brief Wondrous Life of Oscar Wao*. He is fiction editor of *Boston Review*.

Tananarive Due, an American Book Award and NAACP Image Award recipient, won the 2017 British Fantasy Award for her collection *Ghost Summer*. She teaches at UCLA and Antioch University Los Angeles.

Henry Farrell is professor of political science and international affairs at George Washington University. He is a regular contributor to the *Washington Post*'s Monkey Cage blog.

JR Fenn's writing has appeared in *Gulf Coast*, *DIAGRAM*, *PANK*, *Versal*, *Cosmopolitan*, and the *Atlantic*. She teaches at SUNY Geneseo.

Maria Dahvana Headley is a *New York Times*–bestselling author, editor, playwright, and screenwriter. Her most recent book is *Aerie*.

Nalo Hopkinson has received the World Fantasy, John W. Campbell, Sunburst, and Andre Norton Awards. She is a professor of creative writing at the University of California, Riverside. She is completing *Blackheart Man*, a fantasy novel set in a magical Caribbean past.

Mike McClelland is the author of the fiction collection *Gay Zoo Day*.

Maureen McHugh's first novel, *China Mountain Zhang*, won the James Tiptree Award. Her collection of short stories, *After the Apocalypse*, was one of *Publishers Weekly*'s Ten Best Books of 2011. She teaches Interactive Storytelling at the University of Southern California.

China Miéville is three-time winner of the prestigious Arthur C. Clarke Award and has won the British Fantasy Award twice. His latest book is *October*. He also edits the magazine *Salvage* (http://salvage.zone/).

Jordy Rosenberg is an Associate Professor at the University of Massachusetts-Amherst and author of the forthcoming novel *Confessions of the Fox*.

Peter Ross is a journalist in Glasgow, Scotland. An Orwell Fellow, he is the author of *Daunderlust* and *The Passion of Harry Bingo*.

Sumudu Samarawickrama's work has appeared in *f:oame* and *Overland*, and was shortlisted for the 2017 Judith Wright Poetry Prize. She is co-runner-up for the 2017 Ada Cambridge Poetry Prize.